LP
FIC
Glasb

DARK LEGION

Near the village of Tormount, on Cranston's Hill, Malcolm Amberley had been found dead. He was discovered in the centre of the Standing Stones, clutching the curiously ornamented hilt of a strange dagger, driven into his heart. A curtain of evil hung over the village, a nightmare for Terence Amberley who arrived to attend his brother's funeral. Did Malcolm commit suicide, or did some evil force still remain viable in the area, forcing him towards a mysterious death?

JOHN GLASBY

DARK LEGION

Complete and Unabridged

LINFORD
Leicester

First published in Great Britain

First Linford Edition
published 2009

British Library CIP Data

Glasby, John S. (John Stephen)
  Dark legion - - (Linford mystery library)
  1. Horror tales.
  2. Large type books.
  I. Title II. Series
  823.9'14–dc22

ISBN 978–1–84782–827–9

Published by
F. A. Thorpe (Publishing)
Anstey, Leicestershire

Set by Words & Graphics Ltd.
Anstey, Leicestershire
Printed and bound in Great Britain by
T. J. International Ltd., Padstow, Cornwall

This book is printed on acid-free paper

1

The Grey Shade

The storm that had lain threateningly over the western horizon for most of the night finally broke over the dark countryside a little after three o'clock in the morning. There was a vivid flash of lightning, an explosion of deep-throated sound that cracked at his eardrums even above the sound of the car engine and then the battering of rain on the windscreen.

With an effort, Terence Amberley forced his mind out of the dark, silent depths; knew he had been driving too long without a rest. Easing himself more upright in his seat, he gripped the wheel, peering through the lashing spray where the wipers strove gallantly to clear the glass, the probing headlights rising and falling hypnotically as the car bumped over the uneven road.

He reckoned he was still fifty miles or so from his destination and eased the pressure on the accelerator a little in spite of the sensation of urgent haste that prompted him to do otherwise. In places, the road narrowed so that two cars could pass only with difficulty — not that there had been much traffic on this road at this ungodly hour of the morning.

He had left the motorway behind half an hour before, veering eastwards along narrow, winding roads that seemed to be leading him nowhere in the all-enshrouding wet blackness. He peered at the wavering world which showed in brief, tantalising glimpses whenever the beams of the headlights touched the writhing branches of titan-armed trees or the looming barrier of a tall hedge whenever the road turned abruptly.

At least, he reflected grimly, the weather was now in tune with his mission. Just the sort of prelude to a funeral.

It was still hard to fully believe that his brother was dead. The message left on his telephone had been brief, had told him little, too little for him to know what he might be heading into. There had been an inquest, held two days before, which meant that Malcolm had not died an ordinary death. There were other, curiously worrying aspects that did not add up in his mind,

He tightened his grip on the wheel, spinning it sharply as a sudden bend loomed up out of the rain and the darkness. Better not to clutter up his mind with ideas of what might have happened, better to wait until he reached Tormount, get some of the answers there if he could. Treherne, his brother's life-long friend, who had left that urgent message, might be able to provide them for him.

An hour later, the road dipped sharply. There was a cluster of orange sodium lights at the bottom of the hill. A sign by the side of the road confirmed that this was Tenterton. Not much further to go now.

It had been a long drive and he had been unable to snatch even an hour's sleep before setting out from London. Had it been possible, he would have avoided coming to the funeral. Malcolm was his only brother but they had not seen each other, nor corresponded for more than three years. But he had heard things concerning Malcolm's activities here in this small Midland village set among the hills and far off the beaten track; strange things, which had disturbed him greatly at the time. If any of those odd rumours had been true it might explain, at least in part, some of the mysterious circumstances surrounding his brother's death.

He glanced at his wristwatch. Four-thirty-five. It would be around dawn when he finally arrived. Already there was a pale grey streak just showing along the wooded skyline.

The dawn brightened swiftly as the storm abated. Into vision came the rain-dripping hedges, the slatted gates on either side, opening out into sodden fields with here and there a brief, fragmentary glimpse of a farmhouse, white-roofed, standing at the bottom of a grassy slope.

Tormount came into view over the brow of a low hill. Many of the houses were hidden behind the tall trees with the single, main street running through the village like a pale grey scar on the landscape, climbing the steep rise on the far side beyond the more distant houses. It was almost five years since he had last visited Tormount, but little seemed to have changed much in the intervening years. An isolated backwater, with a history that stretched back for almost twelve centuries, it remained untouched by the outside world, events tending to pass it by rather than altering it.

He drove past the high, stone gates of the manor standing tall and grim at the end of the long avenue of beeches, leaves and branches hanging limply in the still air and made his way through the deserted main street, pulling up in front of the house a hundred yards beyond the ivy-clad tower of the twelfth-century parish church. Wearily, he switched off the ignition, sat for a moment in the sudden quiet that flooded about him.

Then he got out of the car. The nearby church clock chimed the quarter hour. Five-fifteen. It had taken him longer than he had thought. A weakening reluctance held him for a moment as he stood in front of the door, then he pulled himself together and knocked loudly.

At length the door was opened and Ralph Treherne stood there, hair disarrayed, his face strangely unfamiliar and darkened by a stubble of beard. He motioned Amberley inside, closed the door swiftly behind him with an almost furtive motion.

'I'm glad you were able to come so quickly, Terry,' said the other, ushering him into the front parlour. 'I didn't mean you to travel through the night but now you're here it takes a load off my mind. Sit down and I'll get you a stiff drink. You look as if you need one.'

'Thanks.' Terence lowered himself gratefully into the chair near the hearth where the ashes of the previous night's fire still made a feeble attempt at redness, giving out no warmth to his numbed body. He stretched his legs out straight in front of him. 'I gathered from your message that the funeral was to be early this afternoon and I didn't want to arrive in the middle of it.'

The other came back with the drink, waited until Terence had drunk down half of the raw whisky before speaking. 'In the circumstances, I didn't know what to do. I found your present address and telephone number among some of Malcolm's papers and rang you immediately after the inquest. You were out, so I left that message.'

He gave Terence a quick glance, as if searching for encouragement. 'I got the impression from Malcolm that you weren't exactly close during the past few years. He mentioned you once or twice, but that was all.'

'I suppose we've both been pretty busy with our own work and he seemed to prefer to shut himself away down here, going about those odd researches of his.'

Terence noticed the strangely guilty way Treherne's gaze slid away from his at the mention of his brother's work, knew with a sudden certainty that there was more to this than he had at first believed. He was not too tired after the long night journey to know that Treherne, for all his outward appearance of calm, was a very frightened man.

The other took a nervous turn about the room, clutching his glass tightly in his right hand. His slippered feet made little padding noises on the uncarpeted portions of the floor. Finally, he stopped near the window, twitched the heavy curtain aside for a moment and peered down into the street, then let the curtain fall back into place.

'Would you mind telling me how my brother died?' Terence asked, as an uneasy silence fell. 'I presume that, since there was an inquest, something about his death was not straightforward.'

'I'm afraid there were a great many things about Malcolm's death which were far from being straightforward.' Treherne gulped down the remainder of his drink. 'The place where his body was discovered, the way in which he died and perhaps most of all, the very nature of the things he was investigating.'

'I'm afraid I don't understand.' Terence sat back in his chair, feeling a little of the shock return at the other's words.

Treherne sat down, hands between his knees, looking at the empty glass. As he lifted his head, Terence realised how much older the other looked since he had last met him in London. The lines around his eyes and across his forehead were cut much deeper and the hair at his temples was now grey, almost white.

'This is a county of superstition, Terry. It's more deeply rooted here than perhaps anywhere else outside of Cornwall. There are mysteries here that have survived since before the Middle Ages. They've become an integral part of the life here, which not even the efforts of the church can eradicate, though God knows each succeeding vicar has tried. Witchcraft, the raising of the dead, ghosts, the supernatural — call it what you like. It all goes under the one name here — Black Magic.'

'And you believe that Malcolm was somehow caught up in this?' Had the other not been so serious, the idea would have seemed laughable.

'I know he was. Not in the sense you mean it. His was a strictly scientific investigation of the old legends. He was trying to prove something — the continued existence of evil down the centuries.' He paused impatiently. 'No, don't look at me like that. I know his death has been a shock to me, but I also know what I'm saying. This place reeks of evil. Nowhere is it more pronounced than among the standing stones on the outskirts of the village where your brother's body was found four days ago.'

'Go on,' said Terence as the other hesitated. 'What happened?'

'He must have gone up there late at night, probably looking for something. He was convinced there were peculiar psychic forces still present there, used to spend hours wandering around, poking among those stones. When he hadn't returned the following morning, I decided to go and look for him. There are some dangerous potholes in the area. In the dark a man could quite easily fall and break a leg.'

Terence sensed that the other was finding it difficult to get to the point.

'I found him easily enough. He was

lying face-downward in the middle of the circle of stones. I thought at first he had fallen, hit his head and knocked himself out. Then I turned him over and — It was horrible. I never want to see a face like that again for the rest of my life. But it wasn't just that. There was a knife driven into his chest, clear up to the hilt and his fingers were still clenched tightly around the haft.'

'You mean he had killed himself?' Amberley sat back, astonished, shocked.

Treherne stared fixedly at him. 'You knew Malcolm as well as I did. He'd never take his own life.'

'Then what are you trying to say? That he was murdered?'

'The coroner didn't think so. It was mentioned briefly, as a possibility, but dismissed almost at once. There was too much evidence against it. The only prints on the knife were his own and Doctor Harmon testified that he had died almost immediately and it would have been virtually impossible for anyone to have placed his fingers around the knife as they were found. Then too, there was the question of footprints.

'It had been raining early that night and the ground there was muddy, leaving clear prints. There were only Malcolm's anywhere in the vicinity, apart from mine, of course.'

'Then it seems an open and shut case,' Terence said, pouring himself another drink. The room had brightened now as the dawn changed from a pale grey to yellow. Although Terence had warned himself to stay alert, the strain of the night was reaching him now.

'I wish I could be as sure of that as the coroner was,' retorted the other, rising. 'But there are so many loose ends to this case which no one seems able to tie up. Apart from the fact that Malcolm was not the kind of man to commit suicide, the knife was never satisfactorily explained. I'd never seen it before and I knew your brother better than most. If he had had it in that bizarre collection of his, I would have noticed it. I'm certain of that. No, Terry, I've had plenty of time to think about this case and I'm more convinced than ever that your brother was murdered.'

'You are surely not trying to tell me that someone could have stabbed him to death and not only left no clues, but did it so that all of the evidence pointed to suicide?'

Treherne smiled thinly. 'I don't blame you for being sceptical about this entire affair. But you haven't been as close to it as I have all these years. In a way, I suppose, I saw this coming a long time ago, but there was nothing I could do about it. I think he discovered something during his later researches, something that eventually dominated his mind, made him drive that dagger into his heart.'

'Oh, come now.' Terence walked over to the window looking out over the rain-soaked fields. He could see a narrow lane winding between tall hedges, climbing over the brow of a distant hill and on top of the smoothly-rounded crest, standing out starkly against the dawn sky, tall stone columns which lifted their incongruous bulk to the heavens as if in defiance of Man and of God. It was up there he knew, that Malcolm had met his death.

'You don't believe me.' There was no

emotion in Treherne's voice. 'But remember that this isn't London. We're a lot closer to the old things here than in the city. Those of us who are wise enough to see things as they are and not how we would like them to be, can often sense these overtones of evil. Your brother did, on many occasions before his death.'

'I didn't say that I don't believe you, but good God man, this isn't the Dark Ages.'

'I agree.' The other moved towards the door. 'I hope you will be able to stay on in Tormount a few days after the funeral. I think you may change your mind about a great number of things if you do.' He looked at Amberlev searchingly for a moment. 'Naturally, you must stay here until the funeral, at least. I'll show you the spare room upstairs.'

★   ★   ★

Terence clenched his fingers around the handle of the car door as they entered the iron-barred gateway of the small cemetery. The beeches stood tall and dark and dripping with rain. The funeral cortège

14

had halted in front of the ivy-clad church. He opened the door of the car, got out, his eyes on the silent rows of moss-blotched tombstones, cold and grey in the ravelling mist.

Treherne came around the rear of the car and together they walked over the loose gravel chips. The thin, drifting mist that had risen during the early afternoon clung wraithlike around the slender trunks of the trees and seeped with a cold, clammy touch through his overcoat, embracing and muffling the whole of the churchyard.

The coffin was lifted from the back of the hearse and carried slowly along the narrow, winding pathway, between two of the tall beeches, to the small plot of ground where the freshly-dug grave yawned in the wet, dismal earth.

The Reverend Ventnor stood with his head lowered, scarcely glanced up as the small procession approached. Carefully, the coffin was lowered into the grave, the ropes thrown with a dull rattle on top of the polished wood and gleaming brass.

Amberley stood with his hands clasped loosely in front of him, glancing at the other mourners out of the corner of his eye. He recognized a few of the villagers, their features inscrutable; Doctor Harmon, grey-haired, looking older than his fifty-seven years. There were other men there whose faces meant nothing, opened no doors of memory in his mind.

They stood in an uneasy group around the edges of the grave. Amberley felt the mist clogging the back of his throat, suppressed the desire to cough. The vicar stepped forward to the head of the open grave, the book in his hands, a purple marker lying limply across the open page. He began to speak softly, yet with a vibrant timbre that made his words easily heard by all present.

'Man that is born of woman has but a little time to stay on Earth for his days are numbered and even in the midst of life, we are in death. Yet the Lord has promised that on the Day of Judgment shall we all be raised up, the graves shall open and let forth their dead and all men shall be judged according to their works. For that which thou sowest on Earth, so shall thou reap.'

Amberley heard the other's words as though from a great distance. Standing there, it was as if he was an interloper here, had no part in this funereal ceremony. Dirt and stones rattled briefly and hollowly on top of the coffin. The sound cut through the mist-muffling stillness. Someone nearby coughed, shuffled their feet in the wet earth and leaves.

Ventnor's voice came again, as strong and monotonous as before: 'Ashes to ashes, dust to dust. We now commend the body of this, our brother departed, to the earth from whence he came, in the sure and certain knowledge that God, in his infinite mercy, will forgive those sins of his on Earth and raise up his soul unto eternal life. Amen.'

Amberley switched his gaze to where Treherne stood a few feet away, his head downcast, staring into the open brown gash in the earth. His eyes had the fixed, half-seeing look of a man in a daze, unaware of what was going on around him. Then, as the gravedigger moved forward, dragging his spade over the dirt, he lifted his head with an obvious effort. Amberley saw the sudden gust of expression that flashed over the other's saturnine features, saw him flinch and struggle to steady himself.

For a second, he thought that it was simply the knowledge that Malcolm lay down there, encased in that coffin, which had brought the look of horror to the other's face. Then he saw, with a sudden shock, that Treherne was not looking down into the grave, but over the vicar's stooped figure, in the direction of the mist-shrouded trees on the far edge of the graveyard. Turning his head, he followed the other's fear-filled glance. Everything seemed suddenly deathly still.

Nothing. Just the writhing mist and the dark, shifting outlines of the trees. Yet he could have sworn that he had seen something. He shuddered and felt the muscles of his stomach contract painfully. There was something out there!

But in God's name what was it? Something was drifting among those trees, something curiously formless, as if a patch of the mist was trying to shape itself into human form. There was a sharp tingling at his temples, increasing until he could feel it physically. Standing rooted to the spot, his limbs dead, he stared at the figure which now stood on the edge of the open stretch of ground, his body functionless, his breath stopped up in his chest, incapable of doing anything but stare at the form in helpless shock.

Vaguely, he was aware of Treherne's sharp intake of breath, knew the other was seeing it as clearly as he was. Fingers clenched, nails biting into the flesh of his palms, he found it impossible to withdraw his gaze. It was undoubtedly a man standing there, his face a blur of white beneath some kind of hood, eyes so deep-set that they seemed mere holes in a skeletal face.

Treherne's muttered cry was short and feeble — a mere strangling sound deep in his throat, lost in the clatter of dirt as the grave was filled in. With an effort, Amberley wrenched his neck around, looked into the other's white, shaking features. In spite of the damp chill in the air, sweat stood out on Treherne's forehead, trickled down his cheeks. He squeezed his eyes shut, screwing them up tightly before opening them once more, then drew the back of his hand across his face.

Doctor Harmon's voice broke in on Terence's tumbling thoughts. 'Are you feeling all right, Treherne?'

'What? Oh, it's you, Doctor.' Treherne shook himself visibly. 'Yes, I think so. Must have been the strain.'

'You don't look too well either, Mister Amberley,' said Harmon sympathetically. 'Maybe you had both better come along with me. I understand you drove here through the night. I'll let you have a sleeping draught. You seem all in.'

'Thank you, Doctor.' Terence made an immense effort to recover himself. His hands were shaking by his sides and he forced them to steady. All the time he was looking at the doctor, listening to him, he was calling upon every nerve in his body to turn his head and look back at the trees, knowing he would get no rest unless he did. But when he finally succeeded in looking, there was nothing there. Only the mist seemed a little thicker near the tall, slender trunks than elsewhere in the churchyard.

He let Harmon take his arm and lead him away from the spot, with Treherne following close behind. They passed beneath a stone archway to where the cars were waiting. While he stood hesitantly, Harmon went to where the driver stood, his collar turned up against the clammy mist, spoke briefly to him. The man nodded understandingly, threw Terence a curious glance, then climbed in behind the wheel.

'I've told him to take us straight to my surgery,' Harmon explained, crushing into the seat beside him. 'I don't imagine you feel like talking to all of the others just now. This tragic affair must have come as a shock to you. I knew your brother well. A strange man in some ways, perhaps a little eccentric, but in spite of this, he fitted well into the community,'

'I get the impression though, that the research he was doing was looked upon, not only as highly eccentric, but dangerous too.'

'Dangerous . . . ?' repeated the other, with a quick glance in Treherne's direction. 'I'm afraid I don't quite understand.'

'Surely it's obvious,' Terence blurted out. 'Ever since I got here, I've had the feeling that people firmly believe that whatever it was he was seeking finally destroyed him.'

'As a doctor,' said Harmon, 'may I give you a piece of advice? Don't start getting ideas like that into your head. Much as I hate to say it, your brother committed suicide. The fact that he was found up there among the Standing Stones means nothing.' He paused, then went on more seriously: 'I did not mean to tell you this, not so soon anyway, but your brother was a very sick man.'

'Nonsense,' muttered Terence sharply, speaking a little more harshly than he had intended. 'Malcolm never had a day's serious illness in his life.'

'This was not a physical illness,' said the doctor gently.

'Are you trying to tell me he was insane?'

Harmon looked momentarily uncomfortable. There was clearly something he felt he had to say, but was finding it difficult. Eventually, as the car turned off the main street, he said: 'Let's simply say that his intense fascination with these old legends gave him fits of depression, sometimes bordering on paranoia My belief is that he took his own life during one of these bouts of mental aberration. I think you would be well advised to leave it that way and not go probing more deeply into these things.'

'I wish I could believe that,' said Terence as he got out of the car.

'You *must* believe it.' There was a peculiar insistence in the other's tone. 'The dead are dead. Better to let them lie in peace.' He walked ahead of them and unlocked the door of the surgery.

As he moved to follow him, Terence threw a quick look at Treherne, felt a slight shock as he noticed the look of fright on the man's face. Tiny beads of perspiration glistened on his brow. But there was no time to question him about his fears for at that moment Harmon said. 'Now that your brother has been buried, Mister Amberley, may I ask if you intend to remain long in Tormount?'

'That depends on a great many things,' Terence said slowly.

'Such as?' The other snapped the question harshly.

'Let's just say that there are some questions about my brother's death which still haven't been answered.'

'But surely the inquest — ' began the other.

Terence shook his head. 'If there's one thing I've learned about official inquests it's that they always try to find the logical explanation for anything, utterly disregarding everything else.'

'And you think that there is something else?' Harmon's sideways glance took in Treherne as well as Terence.

'The more I hear about this affair, the more positive I am about that.'

The doctor seemed on the point of making a sharp retort, then turned on his heel and went into the back room. Treherne spun on Amberley. 'Why on earth did you have to say that? It was mainly on Harmon's evidence that the coroner reached his verdict.'

'Perhaps,' Terence nodded. He could feel the tightness growing in his mind. 'But you don't believe any more than I do that Malcolm killed himself because his mind was unhinged.'

'What does it matter what I believe?' Treherne shrugged. 'The whole of the village wants to believe it and if you start dragging up these old things you'll only make matters much worse. Take Harmon's advice and let the dead sleep in peace.'

Harmon came back into the room. He handed a small bottle to Terence. 'Take two of these half an hour before retiring,' he said in his professional voice. 'They'll ensure that you get a good night's sleep. In the morning, I'm sure you will see things in a far different light.'

Terence took the bottle, slipped it into his overcoat pocket. 'I'm sure you mean well, Doctor. I have no wish to remain here any longer than is absolutely necessary, but first I must find out the truth behind what happened.'

'The truth,' Harmon sighed, running the fingers of his right hand through his greying hair. 'How will you know the truth when you find it? You sound very much as your brother did when he came here many years ago. He wanted to discover the truth — and what happened to him?'

'Exactly! What did happen?' Terence looked across the room to where Treherne was standing by the fireplace. 'I think you know a lot more about that than you've told me so far, Ralph.'

Treherne spun on his heel with a sudden, almost frightened, movement. 'You're not trying to blame me for his death, are you?'

'No. But I'll swear that there's something unutterably evil here and you are aware of it. I saw — *something* — back there in the graveyard. You saw it too, so there's no use in denying it. Standing over by the trees near the fields.'

'I — I didn't see anything,' Treherne said falteringly. 'It was just the whole atmosphere of the place, the mist and the cold and . . .'

Harmon looked momentarily perplexed, then he said tightly to Terence, 'Just what did you see, Amberley?'

'I'm not sure. I noticed Ralph staring fixedly over the vicar's shoulder and turned to see what he was looking at. It was misty in that direction, but I'll swear there was a figure standing there just beneath the trees. It looked like a man but — '

'There was nothing there I tell you.' Treherne seemed almost beside himself. He started forward, one hand held in front of him. 'I saw nothing!'

'Very well, you saw nothing,' Terence said softly. 'But I definitely saw there was something there. Whether it has anything to do with what has been going on around here, I don't know. But this is just one of the reasons why I intend to stay and find out. Someone is deliberately trying to hide something and since it was my brother who died, you can't blame me for wanting to find out what it is.'

Curiously neither man attempted to argue in the face of his determination. Finally, Harmon said quietly: 'You'd better get some rest, Amberley, Whatever it is that's troubling you will take on a calmer light in the morning.' He led the way to the door, paused as he opened it.

'Just one word of advice. Your brother seemed intent on pursuing these old, and often curious, legends about Tormount and the surrounding countryside. It became a mania with him. Whatever you do, try not to let what you fancied you saw this afternoon become such an obsession with you. The mist can play strange tricks with the imagination. And just take two of those tablets. They're quite strong and an overdose could be dangerous.'

'I'll remember, Doctor.' Terence gave a brief nod, followed Treherne out into the drizzling mist.

During the walk back through the village, both men were silent, engrossed in their own private thoughts: Treherne inwardly terribly afraid and Amberley sensing, in some odd way, the chill that was rising within him towards some approaching summit of horror.

2

The Coming of the Fear

Terence retired early that night. The long drive to Tormount, coupled with the curious, macabre events of the afternoon, had tired him more than he had realised. His room overlooked the rear of the house and for a moment, after undressing, he slipped into the warm dressing gown which Treherne had provided and stood in front of the window with the room light extinguished, staring out into the night.

The air had become appreciably colder and with the rising of the moon, a couple of days after full, the mist had dissipated completely, leaving the air crystal clear. The quickening shafts of brilliant moonlight threw the nearby groups of trees into harsh shadow and it was as if the entire countryside was holding its breath in a deathly hush, not a branch stirring, nothing moving as far as the eye could see. It was a silence and a stillness; but not a calm tranquillity. The air of utter malevolence that he had sensed since his arrival in the village was still there, hanging like an invisible shroud over the fields and the narrow, moonlit lane that ran past the edge of the house towards the low rise of the distant fields.

Off to his left, he could just make out the squat tower of the church, gleaming spectrally, its long shadow falling slant-wise over the graveyard that nestled at its foot. The stunted teeth of the tombstones shone in the flooding moonlight and the mere sight of them sent a shiver of superstitious fear coursing through his veins.

Why, he wondered, had Treherne lied about what they had both witnessed that afternoon? Was he afraid to speak out for fear of being called a fool, or perhaps being considered insane? He could not help recalling some of Doctor Harmon's words to him and it came to him that there might have been a hidden meaning to them. Maybe the other sincerely believed that Malcolm had been mad, had wanted to warn him that insanity was sometimes hereditary and that if he continued to probe into things which did not concern him, there was a chance that he, too, might become similarly unbalanced in his outlook.

He was suddenly thankful that from his window, it was impossible to see those tall stone pillars that stood atop Cranston's Hill. The moon drifted suddenly behind a thick bank of cloud and it was as if a black curtain had abruptly descended. The desire to climb into bed and forget, for the night at least, the uncomfortable chaos of his thoughts, was strong within him, but some imp of perverseness held him at the window, waiting impatiently for the moon to reappear.

In the morning, he decided he would talk with some of the people in the village. He remembered several of them from his visits here that had, until some years before, been fairly frequent. Then, there had been no inkling of the horror that was one day to come. Maybe he would find someone willing to talk to him about Malcolm.

The clouds parted raggedly, the moon came out again, shining serenely over the deserted countryside. No, not quite deserted! A sudden movement caught and held his attention. The lane which led past the side of the house, branched about a hundred yards away, one narrow pathway leading to the house on the side of the hill, a house which had once belonged to his brother and which was now in total darkness. Somehow, he had not felt up to going there that afternoon following the funeral to check over Malcolm's belongings. Now a slight figure was walking quickly towards the house. A few moments passed before he recognised the dark figure.

Anne Cowdrey. What on earth was she doing out there at this ungodly hour?

She and Malcolm had been very close, he remembered. Indeed, he had often thought that the two of them might have married someday, had joked with Malcolm about his backwardness in asking her to be his wife. Strangely, he had not seen her among the mourners at the funeral.

Whether the strain had proved too much for her and she had been unable to face the ordeal, he did not know.

He watched the slight figure until the girl had turned out of sight along the lane leading up to the house.

Without warning, a light suddenly appeared in one of the lower windows of the distant house. For a long moment, he stared at it as though hypnotised. Then Anne must have a key to the place. But why had she gone there at this time of the night, alone? How long he stood at the window, it was impossible to estimate. Perhaps half an hour passed before the light was extinguished and some fifteen minutes later, he saw Anne's dark figure, the high collar pulled up around her head, come back along the lane. He thought that she glanced up at his window as she passed but could not be sure that this was not a trick of the moonlight.

After she had gone, he sank down on to the bed and realised that he was shaking all over.

★ ★ ★

Ralph Treherne sipped his coffee slowly, staring at Terence over the rim of the cup. 'I'm afraid I no longer have keys to the house, Terry,' he said tightly. 'The police took them when they locked the place up a few days ago.'

'I'd better have a word with them then.' It had been on the tip of his tongue to mention Anne Cowdrey's nocturnal visit to his brother's place, but now he thought better of it. It was just possible that there might be some logical explanation.

'You'll want to go through his effects, naturally,' The other finished his coffee. 'Then I suppose the house will go up for sale. But you may not find it easy to get a buyer for it. Since his death, that place seems to have gained a bad reputation. You know how these country people like to talk.'

Terence leaned back in his chair. 'I was also thinking of looking up Anne Cowdrey. Is she still living here?'

'Anne? Why, yes. She took Malcolm's death very badly. They were extremely close friends as you know. We all thought . . . well, that one day the two of them might marry.' He got to his feet. 'I'd be careful what you say to her. She's a highly strung girl and the shock has come as a terrible blow to her.'

'I'll be very discreet,' Terence promised. He glanced out of the window. The pale wintry sunlight gleamed wanly over the street, glimmering on the frosty fields. A glance at his watch told him it was almost ten o'clock. 'Well, there's no time like the present. I'll call in at the police station on my way.'

'Would you like me to come with you?' asked the other.

Amberley shook his head, 'I think I'd better do this my own way.'

Leaving the house, he made his way along the quiet street, feeling the biting chill of the wind, even through the thickness of his overcoat. The police-sergeant seated behind the desk regarded him in puzzlement, then his expression changed as he obviously recognised him.

'It's Mister Amberley, isn't it?' He leaned forward. 'Sorry I didn't recognise you at first, sir, but it's been some years since you were last here, hasn't it?'

Terence nodded. 'I'm only sorry I didn't manage to get down more often. If I had, I may have been able to prevent this terrible tragedy.'

'I wouldn't blame yourself too much, sir. We can't possibly foresee these things.' The other seemed anxious for conversation and Terence guessed that very little happened to disturb the even tenor of a village policeman's life.

'Did you know my brother well?' he asked, seating himself at the sergeant's gesture.

'As well as most, I'd say. He was, if you don't mind my saying so, a very queer bird. I'm not a Tormount man myself, come from Nottingham. But I pride myself on keeping an open mind on these strange legends. Not, mind you, that I believe in them as your brother obviously did, but most of the villagers simply refuse to talk about them and I used to have several long discussions with Malcolm Amberley whenever he was in the mood to talk.'

Terence sat forward, suddenly interested. 'What sort of things did he talk about, Sergeant . . . ?'

'Sergeant Willingham, sir.' The other smiled warmly. 'He used to badger the vicar to let him go through the old records locked away in the church vaults. Seems there were a lot of peculiar things written about five or six hundred years ago about what went on in Tormount in those days. They used to perform odd rites up there on Cranston's Hill where the Standing Stones are. Your brother was convinced that Black Magic was carried out, that they used to worship the devil on top of the hill on certain nights of the year, make human sacrifices on some carved stone altar that used to be in the middle of the stone pillars. It isn't there now, of course, and there's nobody still living in the village who can remember a time when it was, but the records speak of it so I suppose he was right on that point.'

'I see,' mused Terence. He shivered inwardly as if an icy finger had been suddenly laid along his back.

'I'm sure that the trouble was,' went on the other quietly, 'that he went a lot further than that. He seemed to think that whatever evil was brought into being in those days, still lives on in some form or other, in the village. I tried to get him to talk about this, but what he said seemed vague and he used terms I couldn't understand. He once said that it was possible certain people in Tormount might be *en rapport* with those evil villagers of those days so that the vibrant force was still able to exist, independently of those who originally brought it up out of the Pit.'

Terence started in spite of himself.

'Do you know what he meant by that, sir?' asked the other pointedly.

'I think so. He obviously thought that there was some spiritual link between the people who worshipped the devil in those days, and people who are alive today.'

'Doesn't really make sense, does it?'

'I wish I could be absolutely sure of that. However, the real reason I came was to see if I could have the keys to my brother's house. I understand that it was locked up by the police before the inquest.'

'Yes, that's right.' The sergeant heaved

his not inconsiderable bulk out of the chair and moved to the rear of the office. 'We thought it best to do that until you arrived. Very often, after a case like this, we get sightseers around, full of morbid curiosity, ready to pick up any little things they can lay their hands on. Besides, there could be something of value among your late brother's possessions.'

He came back and handed the bunch of keys over. Then he pulled out a large, stiff-backed book, coughed apologetically. 'If you could just sign for them, sir. It's just a formality but the superintendent insists on it.'

'I understand.' Terence wrote his name in the space that the other indicated then took the keys, thanked the sergeant, and left.

Old legends and records, sacrificial murders on top of Cranston's Hill, a graven altar set in the centre of the stones . . . Although he now knew something of what Malcolm had been digging into these past few years, it still did not give him any concrete evidence that his brother's death was anything but the suicide that the coroner had stated it to be.

He turned along the short lane that eventually led him through a small wicker gate, across a wide lawn, to the charming house that stood facing the spacious grounds.

He rang the bell and waited. The sane, everyday sound of a tractor moving along the edge of one of the nearby fields, reached his ears and occasionally a faint shout would drift down to him on the wind. The village was going about its normal duties.

Anne opened the door, stared at him in surprise for a moment, then she smiled. 'Terry! Come inside.' She led the way into the front room with its vase of late chrysanthemums in the window and another of red roses on the table.

'Father's out at the moment, but he should be back soon . . . ' She broke off. Her tone was graver and when she went on: 'This is a terrible affair, Terry. I really don't know what to say. The day before it happened, he seemed so alive, so excited at some discovery he had made.'

'Then you don't believe it was suicide?'

She shook her head miserably. 'I don't. But we can't go against the evidence at the inquest. His fits of depression, alternating with periods of almost uncontrollable excitement. At times, he was so strange that he frightened me.'

'I've had a talk with Sergeant Willingham. He told me something of Malcolm's work. Surely he wasn't so foolish as to actually believe all of this nonsense of black magic, calling up the devil on top of Cranston's Hill and the raising of the dead?'

'I'm afraid he did. He was absolutely convinced of the authenticity of those happenings. Whenever he used to talk about it, he made it all sound so real that you couldn't help agreeing with him. Over the past few months, I've been assailed by such a feeling of evil, like some terrible, unseen presence. I know Malcolm was aware of it; a sense of something horrible which kept growing all the time.'

'And you think it may have had something to do with his death?'

'I'm not sure. I went along to the inquest. I had to give evidence, you see.'

'And do you agree with the verdict that was reached?'

'In the circumstances, there was no other verdict that could possibly be reached,' she muttered defensively.

'Yet you don't believe it was the right one.' It was more of a statement than a question.

She nodded her head helplessly. 'There are so many things that have happened since Malcolm started digging into those old records in the church, things which I can't possibly begin to explain. Oh, Terry!' She came closer to him, caught at his arm. 'I'm scared. There have been times when I was sure I would go mad.'

A pause, then she went on in a hoarse whisper. 'I've *seen* things, Terry. Awful things. Oh, I haven't dared to tell anyone else about them. No one would believe a single word of it.'

'Maybe if you were to tell me it would help. Better not bottle all of this up inside you.'

'It was about eight weeks ago. Malcolm

had found some passage in the records that he had succeeded in translating, something which threw him into a veritable fit of excitement. He was sure that the main ceremonies which were held in the early Middle Ages took place on Cranston's Hill on May Eve and again at Halloween. He had made up his mind to go up there on All Hallows Eve and spend the night among the Standing Stones. He asked me to go with him, mainly because he wanted to have an independent witness with him just in case anything did happen. It was a foolish thing to do, I know. But I felt certain that in his state of mind, he could imagine anything.'

'So you went with him?'

She nodded, a look of horror in her eyes as though remembering terrible events. 'I thought I was just humouring him, going up there that night. There was a moon, but a strong wind made it extremely cold. We got to the top about half an hour before midnight and settled down near one of the Standing Stones. I don't know if you've ever been up there,

Terry. But at night, especially in the moonlight, there's something eerie and strange about that place.

'Malcolm had taken a small cine-camera with him and a portable tape-recorder — '

'Didn't he have more modern equipment?' Terence questioned, surprised.

Anne shrugged. 'He'd bought it cheaply from the widow of a one-time cine-enthusiast. He said it was ideal for his purposes. After we had set these up, we just sat there on one of the fallen stones and waited.' She paused, then went on a trifle shakily: 'It must have been close on midnight when we first heard something. I can't really describe it, some curious vibration in the air, as if voices were speaking from somewhere very far away, muffled and altered as though by some great bell tolling just at the limit of audibility. It was as if the vibration was driving its way into my body, not only through my ears, but through every pore. Malcolm had started up the tape-recorder and was on the point of moving across to the camera on its tripod when it suddenly tilted, seemed to jump into the air as though something had deliberately struck it with a great deal of force. Something unseen but terrible descended on us. I can't describe it. It was sheer, unadulterated evil, sudden and overwhelming.'

'You didn't get any sense of direction from which it was coming?' Terence asked.

'No. It just seemed to swamp down and swallow us up completely. Malcolm felt it too, but I think he seemed to have been expecting it. But that wasn't the worst.' Her voice, which had gradually dropped to a mere whisper, rose again. 'I think it started with a mist in the middle of the circle, but it was no ordinary mist. It kept twisting and forming itself into shapes.'

'What sort of shapes?' he asked sharply. Yesterday, he had seen an odd shape that had appeared compounded of mist.

Anne looked at him curiously for a moment, then said tightly: 'Some of them were like men and women, oddly bowed, moving around in a wide circle but keeping among the Standing Stones. But there were others — '

'Others?' Amberley was aware of the sudden tightening in his chest.

'Shapes that weren't even remotely human! I think I must have fainted for a time. The next thing I knew, Malcolm was helping me back down the hillside, telling me it was all right, that it was just something we had imagined up there.' She shivered convulsively. 'But it wasn't. Whatever it was, it was as real as you or I.'

So there *was* something undeniably evil here in this quiet country village, something his brother had been on the track of and which had almost certainly been the cause of his death. He knew at that moment that he would not possibly be able to leave Tormount without getting to the bottom of this mystery.

Abruptly, he changed the subject: 'I saw you go out to Malcolm's house late last night, Anne. I didn't know you had a key.'

'Why yes. I used to help Malcolm with his cataloguing and typing. He gave me one some time ago.' She got to her feet, made her way across the room and came back with it. 'I went there last night hoping I might be able to find something that would throw some light on his death.'

'And did you?'

'No. I thought perhaps I might find the camera, or the tape. That, at least would give me some proof of what actually happened.'

'I think the sooner I look over the place, the better.' He smiled faintly. 'That was the reason I got the keys from Sergeant Willingham. I don't suppose I could persuade you to come with me? After all, you know the house far better than I do.'

'I'd be glad to help. I'll leave a note for Dad just to stop him worrying. This business has hit him hard. He liked Malcolm a lot.'

★　★　★

Their footsteps echoed in the long, dusty hall. The smell of the abandoned house lay all around them, getting into their nostrils as they made their way into the library, which opened off to one side of the central stairway.

'This is where Malcolm did all of his work.' Anne said, an expressive sweep of her right arm taking in the whole room. 'I thought there might be something here, but I could find nothing.'

'Let me see.' Slowly, he made his way along the long shelves of books. Many seemed incredibly old, priceless first editions in their original bindings. Some were almost devoid of any title on the outer cover, others could just be read and no more. Yet he saw enough to tell him the sort of research that his brother had been doing during the years he had lived in Tormount.

'Have you found something?' Anne came and stood beside him, looking down at the book in his hand.

'I must confess I never expected to find this,' he said in a low voice. 'As far as I know, the only other copy in the country is kept under lock and key in a special room at the British Museum.'

'The *Daemonomicon*,' murmured the girl. 'What does it mean? I've never seen this volume before.'

'I'm quite sure it isn't the kind of thing he would parade in front of anyone,' said Terence with a shudder. 'I've heard vaguely of it, but I never thought I'd be ever holding a copy in my hand.' He turned the stained, yellowed pages. The corner of one of the pages had been turned down and a passage marked in the margin.

Terence carried the book over to the window, held it to the light and began to read:

''The land which lies to the north of the village of Tormount has long been known to be accursed. In particular, the area known as Cranston's Hill is the reputed centre of satanic activities surpassing even those of Thurnley Abbey and High Tor in Devon. The Standing Stones are of great antiquity, dating from prehistoric times but it was during the late thirteenth century that the first stories of magical rites became rife throughout the countryside.

''The folklore associated with these evil practices and particularly with the family of the de Grinleys, landowners and lords of the manor, continued for more than four centuries during which time, various witch-trials were carried out, resulting in the burning of at least thirty men and women accused of selling their souls to the Devil and participating in the inhuman and blasphemous iniquities centered around the Standing Stones. The last of the great wizards was Richard de Grinley (1642 —) whose death was never recorded.

' 'The legends associated with this man are many and well-documented, including his ability to raise and converse with the evil powers, the raising of the dead and his prophecy that he would never die so long as the Altar of Belial remained in the village.' '

'What can it all mean?' Anne asked in an awe-struck tone. 'How can anyone live all of this time?'

'They can't,' said Terence fiercely. 'This is just another of those old village legends. But that doesn't mean, unfortunately, that there isn't any evil still present. Evil can exist in many forms, but it nearly always needs some focus on which to fasten itself.' He tightened his lips, replaced the book on the shelf. 'It's rather like magnetism. You need the poles of a magnet before you can get a magnetic field. You can't see the field once you've generated it. But you can see the tremendous effects it can have on pieces of iron. An evil force is much the same. You need a pole so that it may be generated, very often as in the case of poltergeists someone who isn't even aware that they are the cause of the phenomenon.'

'How horrible.' She shuddered, turned away. 'I've never heard of the de Grinleys. They must have owned the manor in those days. Perhaps Lady Parrish may know of them.'

'We can ask her. But first I'd like to take a further look around here. If, as you say, Malcolm took a cine-camera and a tape-recorder up on top of Cranston's Hill that night, then my guess is he would waste no time in developing the film and playing back the tape. He isn't likely to have destroyed such valuable pieces of evidence, so they have to be around here someplace. Not that he would leave them in full view for anybody to find.'

A thorough search of the library revealed nothing. There were many more books whose half-obliterated titles both intrigued and frightened Terence, but he did not waste time going through them. At the moment, he was far more interested in finding more concrete evidence of what was going on in and around Tormount.

The kitchen was nothing remarkable, nor were most of the other rooms, although they all bore the unmistakable stamp of a man's touch, there being nothing feminine about them.

They came at length into a large room at the rear of the house. It had the air of having been lived in and Terence looked about him curiously, noticed the door set in the far wall and went over to it, twisting the handle. It was locked.

'Do you know what is behind here, Anne?' he asked.

She shook her head. 'I think it was one of Malcolm's workrooms, but I'm not sure.'

'Maybe one of these keys will fit.' He tried them one after the other. The fourth key turned easily in the lock and pulling open the door, he stepped into the darkened room, left hand fumbling for the light switch. Snapping it on, he looked about him. It was a well-equipped darkroom. Lengths of film had been clipped on to a cord that stretched from one side to the other. There was a stainless steel sink, an enlarger and a projector on a high stand with a permanent screen fixed on to the blank expanse of wall at one side.

Just to one side of the door was a small metal filing cabinet and beyond it, a set of drawers. Pulling open the top drawer, he found it filled with small cardboard boxes, each neatly labelled, each containing a reel of film.

'This may be what we're looking for,' he said with a touch of excitement. Swiftly, he examined the labels on the boxes. Fortunately, his brother had been a tidy, meticulous sort of person and all of the labels were self-explanatory so that he was able to ignore most of the reels at once.

Finally, he was left with three that might be the one he was looking for. All of this time, the girl had been watching him curiously from just inside the doorway.

He threw her a quick glance over his shoulder. 'Would you see if you can find a power point in the room and plug in that projector, Anne?'

Obediently, she picked up the plug, located the point near the door and thrust it in, then walked over to the projector and switched it on. The bright beam of light shone brilliantly on the white screen, forming an intense rectangle of light. It was the work of a few moments to fit the first film into place. Then he switched off the main light and ran the length of film through the projector. It had obviously been taken in broad daylight from a point near the summit of Cranston's Hill, showing a panoramic view of the Standing Stones; great columns of crudely-hewn rock which thrust themselves up from the barren soil, forming a rough circle in the centre of which was a patch of ground in which nothing seemed to grow, like a wide scar in the earth.

'That must be where the altar stood in the middle of the thirteenth century,' he said quietly, his words echoing hollowly in the confined space. 'I wonder when it was removed — and why?'

'Or to where,' put in Anne harshly.

As he stared at the picture that was being unfolded on the flat, rectangular screen, standing quite still beside the softly-whirring projector, he was aware of a deep brooding menace? It was almost as if he were standing on that lonely hilltop, looking out on those pillars of stone. The angle of the scene changed abruptly. The camera had been suddenly tilted downward until it was pointed directly at the ground. For a moment, Terence felt a distinct sense of shock, as though an electric current had sizzled its way through his brain. Malcolm had clearly seen something at that moment which had diverted his attention from the great circle of stones. For a second, the picture was blurred. Then it came into focus with a rush. There were footprints in the muddy earth, which bordered the crest of the hill. An eternity seemed to pass as he stared at the screen, scarcely able to believe his eyes, or force the rapid thudding of his heart into a slower, more normal, pace. Most of the prints were those of bare feet, standing out quite clearly in the mud. But here and there, showing perhaps a little more indistinctly than the others — a fact for which he felt curiously thankful — *were others that were not human*!

He heard Anne's sharp intake of breath, knew she had seen them too. Had they been formed by some animal which had been deliberately taken up there to be sacrificed? It was the only thought that occurred to him. A moment later, the last few frames of the film clattered through the projector and there was only the glaring white light showing on the screen.

A sudden feeling of nausea overtook him, but he forced it away with an effort. He felt the girl move a little closer towards him, her hand on his arm.

'Those strange prints in the mud,' she whispered. 'Did you see them?'

'Just some animal,' he forced himself to

say. 'There's no date on this reel of film, but if Malcolm took it, as I'm sure he did, then it must mean that these hideous rites are still going on up there on top of Cranston's Hill. Those prints couldn't have been much more than a day old when he filmed them. The next shower of rain would have washed them away completely.'

He replaced the reel in its box, ran the second one through. It showed nothing more than a few isolated views of the village, taken from different places. The main theme seemed to be centered on the ancient church. There were one or two sequences shot inside the church itself, mainly very dim pictures because of the poor lighting conditions, so that few of the finer details were visible.

'Nothing much there,' he said, as he put it back. He picked up the last box, turned it over in his hands, noticing that this one, out of all those he had found, did not have any label on it. It had evidently been exposed and processed though and he found his fingers trembling a little as he fitted it into the projector. The feeling of a third presence in that small room was so strong now that he found himself glancing over his shoulder with a nervous apprehension. Shaking off the feeling, he pressed down the projector switch. The screen was dark, almost completely so. Then he felt Anne's fingers clutch his wrist, heard her harsh whisper.

'This is the film, Terry. I'd know it anywhere.'

He held his breath. The lighting was extremely poor but vaguely he was able to make out the great columns of stone as the images flickered across the screen. There was a pale flooding of moonlight but this only served to enhance the darkness rather than diminish it.

'Watch closely!' commanded the girl. Terence felt her body go rigid beside him.

At first, he could see nothing other than the Standing Stones, almost exactly as he had seen them in the first film he had run, although from a somewhat different angle and from a point much closer. Then, without warning, he felt the muscles of his stomach contract painfully.

For there was something there, something seen dimly and oddly distorted as if the camera had been out of focus when the pictures had been taken. He felt his eyes twisting as he tried to make out what he was seeing, but several moments fled before the realisation came to him that those vague images were in focus; it was simply that his mind had been insisting that they had been human figures and was concentrating on looking at them as such; whereas now that his vision had re-orientated itself with a sudden rush of clarity, he saw that there was very little about them which was human at all.

The nausea came back in an over-whelming rush. What fiendish blasphemies were these that had been captured in such faithful detail by the innocent emulsion of the film? It was like a picture drawn from Dante's Hell itself.

Sweat, clammy and cold, commenced to trickle down his back. The scene was terrible and terrifying. There was a mind-engulfing sense of utter disbelief and horror. Had those things been of flesh and blood, he knew he would have lost his senses. As it was, there was some unsubstantial quality about them. He recalled the words that Anne had used only a little while before. Like things shaped out of mist. It was a very good description, but it only did partial justice to the horror of them all.

When the last frame clicked through the projector and the light of the bulb lanced out, blotting out everything, he had to force himself upright, standing with one arm around the girl's waist and the other clinging with a desperate strength to the edge of the small table on which the projector stood. He turned to glance down at Anne's upturned face.

The same look of indescribable horror was there which he knew to be mirrored on his own.

He wiped a shaking hand across his wet forehead, switched off the machine and walked mechanically to the door to put on the room light.

'Do you believe me now?' whispered Anne. Her hand was up to her face, her eyes wide, the pupils dilated. 'If we showed that film to the police they would have to believe us too.'

'No. We can't do that.' He shook his head violently. 'It would prove nothing as far as they were concerned.'

'But those things we saw — ' began the girl.

'Could very easily have been faked by Malcolm. He was an expert photographer and it just isn't true that the camera never lies. No, we have to get more proof, much more, before we can go to them for help.'

'What more can we possibly get?'

'At the moment, I'm not sure. I need some time to think this out. But of one thing I am convinced. Somewhere in this village, there is someone who knows much more of this terrible affair than either you or I. Possibly much more than Malcolm ever guessed or discovered.'

'How can you be so certain of that?'

'Because as I explained earlier, for evil to exist like this there has to be a pole of power, some focus which can not only attract it, but also concentrate it to the point where it can have a separate existence. It may be that we're too late. That whoever, or whatever, this person or object is, is no longer needed. If that should happen to be the case, then God help us all — because nothing else can.'

They locked the house and made their way back along the narrow winding lane and it was not until they had turned the corner and were out of sight of the building that any sense of normality returned to them, that they were able to breathe properly once more and think clearly again. They were halfway along the main street before Anne found her voice again.

'It was real, wasn't it, Terry? I mean we did see those things on that film?'

'We saw them,' he said grimly. 'And they were only too real.'

3

The Standing Stones

Two miles out of Tormount the hills pressed close to the narrow country road and there was something odd and sinister in their aspect, something about the too-rounded summits, which sent a little chill through Terence Amberley's mind as he walked slowly along the deserted road. He had left the main road ten minutes before, striking northward and upward to where Cranston's Hill loomed up on the near horizon, its summit, higher than any of the others by almost a hundred and fifty feet, wreathed in a grey mist that, from ground level, obscured all sight of the Standing Stones.

Anne had begged him to allow her to accompany him but he did not want her with him on this particular occasion; not after what he had seen on that film in Malcolm's darkroom the previous day. It was not a wholesome landscape that he was now entering. The stillness of something very like death hung over the untilled fields and even the hedgerows and small copses that dotted the area, seemed utterly devoid of life. There were no wild creatures around, scurrying through the tangled underbrush, no birds whistling on the branches of the curiously stunted, deformed trees. Even the vegetation which did grow out here was oddly twisted and unnaturally shaped as if nature had decided to run riot and the plants that did grow, sucked an unwholesome nourishment out of the ground.

The road ran through a small grove, the leaves and branches meeting over his head in a thick ceiling of matted green and brown, shutting out the light of the pale, wintry sun. The air under the trees was still and smelled of dampness and decay. Fear had once lurked on Cranston's Hill. Still lurked there if Malcolm had been right and that film had told the truth. Maybe it was nothing more than a tradition, which had been handed down by word of mouth for centuries and written in those old, rotting manuscripts of which Malcolm had talked before he had died. Over the years, a tradition could turn into something more than mere myth, could become so real that its effect on people, particularly simple-minded, superstitious people like these, could be little short of disastrous.

He felt that he would have to discover more about the de Grinley family. There, he was sure, lay the key to the whole mystery. Coming out of the shadow of the grove, he drew in a deep breath of air that seemed suddenly a little purer and cleaner. Leaving the deep gloom behind, he struck out over the ridged brow of the hill, the road gradually degenerating into a track and finally into nothing more than a vaguely-seen scar on the earth where the grass seemed to have been trampled down by countless ages of feet so that it refused to grow with the same unnatural luxuriance as on either side.

Minutes later, he was approaching the wall of mist which shrouded the crest. The sun lost all of its warmth and the chill clamminess closed in on him, seeping into his limbs until they seemed to be moving without conscious volition.

He pulled his coat more tightly about him, turning up the collar. The sun had all but disappeared, glimpsed on rare occasions through the writhing fingers of mist that created a distortion of the rocks and mounds on either side of him, giving them shapes they never really possessed.

How Malcolm and Anne had summoned up sufficient courage to come up to this godforsaken place after dark, with only the pale, spectral moonlight shining over the scene, he would never know. By daylight it was bad enough, but at night, it would be a thousand times worse.

As he clambered over the edge of the ridge, some twenty feet or so below the summit, it was all he could do to resist the urge to turn and make his way back down again, but some dogged sense of persistence kept him moving, barking his shins on out-thrusting fingers of razor-edged stone, feet slipping and sliding over bare patches of treacherous ground.

Finally, panting harshly, he reached the level spot on top of the hill, stood for a long moment simply staring about him, peering into the streamers of mist which parted tantalisingly to reveal scattered glimpses of the tall, grey stones which thrust themselves out of the hard, stony ground like the teeth of some great, antedeluvian monster.

He paced slowly over the uneven ground. There was an air of primal mystery about this place that was due to something more than the mist and the utter stillness. If there was any truth at all in the age-old legends, then those evil men had chosen well to practice their terrible rites up here. He walked around the edge of the great circle, noticing for the first time that the surfaces of the great columns were not merely roughened by time and weather, but bore the traces of age-old inscriptions and carvings, many of an extremely hideous nature.

Giving them but a cursory glance, knowing that his knowledge of ancient writings was not sufficient to enable him either to decipher them or to give a date to them, except perhaps to realise that they were definitely pre-Roman, possibly even pre-Celtic, he moved on into the very centre of the stones. It must have been here that Malcolm had been found. In his mind's eye, he could picture Treherne coming up the hill, hurrying perhaps out of breath, not knowing what he might find, then stumbling upon the prone body of his brother, face-downward on the hard earth, turning him over on to his back only to find that he was dead, with a knife driven deeply into his heart.

The answer to the mystery had to be here, somewhere.

Sweeping his eyes over every visible inch of ground, he noticed at once the bare, empty patch that lay almost at his feet. It was an almost perfect oblong, perhaps ten feet in length and half as much in breadth. Not a single blade of the tough, wiry grass grew within it and going down on to one knee, he ran his fingers over it, grimacing a little as he found that the area was covered with a thin layer of greyish dust.

There was a strange oppressiveness in the atmosphere as if the air were traced with thin, invisible filaments of panic.

There was no sound at all, nothing to tell him that he was not absolutely alone in the place. This was clearly where the old altar had lain. He shuddered to think of all the hapless victims who had been sacrificed on it in days gone by, to appease the old gods, to bring the rain, give better crops, watch over the village and make them victorious over their enemies, when in reality their greatest and most powerful enemy lay within themselves.

A virgin was sacrificed on a stone altar and a day later the rains came to break the drought. Mere superstition?

The initiates howled and danced among the Standing Stones and their enemy's cattle sickened and died. Superstition again? A man delved too deeply into these age-old mysteries, came up to this dreadful place at dead of night and was found stiff and stark the next morning. Superstition? Or was there some terrible power underlying it all? Something that lived and fed on those it nurtured down the centuries?

Getting to his feet, he moved away

from the patch of bare soil. On the point of making his way towards the great circle of stone pillars, he paused as something caught his eye. Slowly, he walked towards it, bent. It was a small hole in the ground, as if the earth had become dislodged and fallen in. Gingerly, he thrust his hand inside, felt cautiously around with his fingers. The hole was deeper than he had anticipated and in the end he was forced to lie flat on his chest and thrust his arm into it as far as it would go. His outstretched fingertips touched something cold and hard. With an effort, he managed to ease it towards him, curl his fingers around it and draw it out.

The object was encrusted with dirt and grime but from its weight, and the dull shine that showed through in places, it was obviously made of some kind of metal. Squatting back on his heels, he took out his handkerchief and began to clean it carefully. Most of the muck and grime fell away easily and he experienced a shock of revulsion as he realised what it was. The slender blade was curved in a strange way and there were curious carvings on the hilt, images very like those that had been graven upon the tall stones of the circle.

'Mr. Amberley?'

The sudden voice, coming from almost directly behind him, made him start. He turned sharply to face the man who had emerged from behind one of the Standing Stones. Then he noticed the other's clerical collar, recognised the Reverend James Ventnor as he advanced towards him.

'I'm sorry if I startled you, but you seemed to be extremely engrossed in something and didn't hear my approach. Besides, the mist up here has that peculiar property of muffling sounds.' He glanced down at the knife in Terence's hands. For a moment there was an expression almost of fear on his bland features, but it was gone quickly.

'I must admit I'm surprised to see a churchman here, Vicar,' Amberley said as he regained his composure.

'Because of its obvious pagan qualities, you mean?' Ventnor smiled faintly. 'No, I simply came because I thought this might be where I would find you. I noticed you leave the village and strike out in this direction. In a tiny community such as ours, the vicar learns much about everyone who comes into the village. People feel that they can always come to him with their troubles and worries.'

'Oh? And some of them, no doubt, are worried by what I'm doing?'

'To put it quite bluntly — yes. They're afraid you may stir up things which, once set in motion, cannot be controlled.'

'I suppose you realise that by saying this, you are as good as admitting that there *are* things waiting to be stirred up.'

'You're a very shrewd man, Mister Amberley. But I admit nothing of the kind. However, there are superstitions that persist in our tiny, isolated community. I can see that you are a very determined man and from somewhere you have got hold of the idea that there is something much more to your brother's unfortunate death, than suicide.'

Terence turned the knife over in his fingers. 'Was it a knife like this my brother used?'

The other hesitated visibly. 'It may have been something like that,' he admitted finally. 'Where did you find it?'

'Buried in the dirt there. Judging from its condition, it must have been there for a very long time.'

'Possibly. If the old records are factual, many strange orgiastic rites were carried out here in the Middle Ages.' The other made no move to examine the knife.

Carefully, Amberley placed the knife in his pocket, fell into step beside the other. He could sense that the vicar was uneasy as they had walked some way down the hillside in silence. Then the other cleared his throat and said: 'Are you sufficiently determined to risk danger to find out what really happened to your brother, Mister Amberley?'

'What sort of danger? The same thing that happened to Malcolm?'

'Possibly.'

Amberley puzzled over the other's sudden change of attitude. How much did he know of this bizarre affair?

'You see, Amberley,' said the other as they reached the road, 'I am a man of

God, but to believe in God, one must also believe in the Devil. Evil is a very real force. If the things that are written in the old testaments in the church are a factual account of what really happened, then there is still potent evil here. Evil capable of destroying a man.'

'Did you warn Malcolm of this?' Terence asked harshly.

The other pointed towards the rounded summit of the hill from which they had just come.

'Malcolm Amberley was a very stubborn man. He came to me about three months before he died with a wild story of the most hideous sort. Vague horrors he had seen on top of Cranston's Hill yonder, grotesque shapes of coagulated nightmare cavorting and dancing among the Standing Stones. Maybe he was looking for help of some kind. Perhaps, if I could have given him some help, he might still be alive today.'

'Then you don't believe the coroner's findings about Malcolm's supposed suicide?'

'I'm sure if my bishop heard me saying

this, he would be extremely shocked. Witchcraft in this day and age! Remember though, that I have seen and experienced nothing. I can only speak from hearsay and from what little I have dared to read of those accursed writings.'

'Perhaps if I might read those old records . . . ' Terence began.

'I keep them locked away,' said the other. His tone was suddenly sharp. 'As I am sure others did before me. However, I am prepared to let you see them just so long as you know what the consequences may be.'

'I understand,' Terence nodded.

The mist was now also forming along the road, obscuring the village a quarter of a mile away. For several moments they trudged in silence, then he turned to the other and said: 'Tell me something, Vicar. Ever since I came to Tormount I've come up against a brick wall whenever I've tried to question people about my brother. Just why are you so helpful now?'

'An ulterior motive, I'm afraid,' confessed the other gravely. 'You see, your brother was not the first person to die in very mysterious circumstances. There have been others and in every case they were unduly interested in Cranston's Hill and the Standing Stones. Your brother had a book in his possession — he lent it to me once but I could not bring myself to read much of it — dealing with this region in the Middle Ages.'

'The *Daemonomicon*.'

'Yes. There were things in there which made me doubt the existence of God, at least of a God of goodness and mercy. Such terrible, revolting incidents. Yet the most frightening thing is that, in spite of my present beliefs, they did explain some of the past happenings. It is difficult to conceive of the full, black power of evil in the midst of our cold, everyday experience.' He rubbed the palm of his hand slowly across his forehead. He was, Terence noticed, perspiring slightly in spite of the sudden chill in the air.

'It seems unbelievable, but the register in the vestry tells of at least fifteen people, men and women, who have died in strange circumstances over the past two hundred and fifty years. The church yonder has stood for almost a thousand years and over the centuries, my predecessors have laboured incessantly to exorcise the village of the demons of darkness that they firmly believed existed here. Yet they failed in their task. Failed dismally.'

★   ★   ★

There was heavy rain that afternoon, and it was not until evening that Terence Amberley was able to move the few things he had brought with him to the house at the end of the long, narrow lane, the house in which his brother had lived for so many years, which housed all that he had lived for and which, Terence felt certain, also held the secret of his death.

Treherne had attempted to dissuade him from going, maintaining earnestly that he could remain with him for as long as he wished but that talk with the Reverend Ventnor had brought a strange sense of urgency to his mind. Now that he had those dusty old records with him, he knew that it would be impossible for him to do anything else but live in the huge, rambling house, set apart from all of the others in the village, until he had got to the bottom of this mystery which lay like a dark shroud over the village.

He had been forced to leave his car in the main street for the path to the house was too narrow to allow him to drive it there. Although his first sight of the house had brought mixed emotions when he had visited it with Anne Cowdrey, now that he saw it for a second time, this remarkable old building slowly assumed a more normal aspect.

As he closed the heavy front door behind him, he wondered what had prompted Malcolm to buy it and live there. Perhaps a desire for absolute privacy while he carried on with his researches into the occult.

As he placed his belongings on the table in the spacious front parlour, Terence caught a whiff of something acrid, rather like incense at the back of his nostrils; a cloying, musty smell that hung unmoving in the air above the familiar smell of dust and mildew.

Switching on the light, he pulled the thick curtains across the wide windows, then built a fire in the hearth, waiting impatiently for the room to warm up before settling down to begin reading through the ancient parish records.

It was a strange and terrible chronicle. Sitting there at night with the wood crackling in the wide ornate hearth and the creaking sounds of the old house all about him, Terence Amberley felt chill upon chill seize him as he continued to read.

Long-winded, often statistical, genealogical as much of the subject matter was, there ran through it all a deep and continuous thread of utter malevolence that impressed him in much the same way as he guessed it had his brother. He knew now why the good vicar kept such a manuscript locked away in the vestry and was so exceedingly loath to allow anyone to read it.

It began wholesomely enough with a history of the de Grinley family, opening amidst a confused maze of dates, the confusion evidently arising from the varied sources available to the author at that time. At first, there was no record of anything sinister connected with the family. William de Grinley had been a favourite of William the Conqueror and for his services had been given the lands around Tormount, south as far as the marshes and north to the meeting of the two rivers. The manor had been built in 1073 and for the next one and a half centuries the village prospered under the de Grinleys.

Then in 1202, sickness came upon the village, wiping out more than half of the population. The pestilence even spread to the crops, which produced curiously abnormal growths and for the first time, witchcraft came to the village. People connected the terror with the great stone monument on top of the hill to the north. Special prayers were said in the church and when these brought no alleviation of the horror that had descended upon them, the ways of God were forsaken. The evil rites began, led in 1223 by a man named Edward Cranston.

Amberley sat quite still in the high-backed chair, the yellowed pages of the ancient manuscript open on his knees, staring into the slowly-dying embers of the fire. At last, the man who had given his name to that accurse place had appeared. Feverishly, he continued reading of this abominable creature, a man horribly deformed, who claimed that only by appeasing the Darker Gods, could the pestilence be removed from Tormount.

Amberley found, as he had half expected, that the de Grinleys now entered into the picture. Hubert de Grinley, only son of Edmond, lord of the manor, entered whole-heartedly into these orgiastic rites. He took to reading — and writing — queer books; initiated the human sacrifices on top of Cranston's Hill, on the huge stone altar in the centre of the Standing Stones. It was not, however, until the death of his father, that Hubert really came into his own. A total of thirty-three victims were murdered during the ritual ceremonies performed during a period of twenty-two years.

The de Grinleys, it seemed, now embarked upon a veritable orgy of terror. The evil madness which had begun with

Hubert continued down the line for more than four centuries, culminating with the much-feared Richard de Grinley whose shocking deeds were too much, even for folk long versed in witchcraft. The plague of some five centuries earlier which had provoked this wave of devil worship had long since been forgotten and with witch hunts in progress throughout the whole of England at this time, the people once more began to return to the fold of the church. Unfortunately, there was no enlightenment in the minds of these superstitious folk and many innocent victims perished during the revolt against the exponents of the Black Art.

There seemed little doubt, according to the manuscript, that Richard de Grinley was both feared and hated at this time. He still retained a few fanatical followers and continued with his blasphemous rites on top of Cranston's Hill, uttering the most terrible curses on the village and there was more talk at this time of inhuman shapes seen among the Standing Stones around the time of full moon, and especially on May Eve and All Hallowes Night.

The royal witch-hunters who roamed the countryside in search of victims seemed to have passed the village by for there was no record of any trials carried out in the vicinity, but in the end, the villagers themselves took the law into their own hands. A band of them, led by the vicar at that time moved against the manor one night during the dark of the moon, dragging out every member of the de Grinley family they could lay their hands on. Brought before the church the next day, they were all condemned to death by burning.

The document ended in much confusion, for Terence could find no mention of Richard de Grinley himself. The author was clearly of the opinion that he had been saved from the stake by his evil masters, those dark monstrosities he had worshipped and served so faithfully and well over the years. Much was made of the curse he was said to have put on the village and the prophecy that he would never die so long as the great altar of Belial remained.

He closed the document, laid it down

on the table beside him. Getting stiffly to his feet, he went over to the window, drew aside the curtain and looked out into the night. The pale moon glimmered behind tattered streamers of cloud and here and there a star showed brightly over the hills. If that taint of evil still lived on out there, surely there should be some way to defeat it, to rid the village of its terrible legacy. He glanced at his watch. It was now well past midnight and the fire in the hearth was no more than a pale glow giving out little warmth.

Shivering, he let the curtain fall into place, then made his way up the wide stairway to the room at the rear of the house. He undressed in the darkness, not bothering to put on the light. His thoughts made him uneasy, disturbed him more than he cared to admit. There were those he knew, to whom witchcraft was merely a quaint and rather fascinating relic of the old days, some survival from the centuries of ignorance when men worshipped things they did not understand. Some even dabbled in it still, attracted by the feeling of power that came from probing into the unknown. Others simply scorned the idea, insisted that it could be explained on the basis of mass hypnotism and a wrong interpretation of the facts.

Until a week or so ago, he had been just such a person, only half-believing in God and utterly denying the possibility of evil being a true and potent force. Now, without warning, he had been plunged into this dark nightmare.

Was this merely an old legend, handed down through the centuries, added to from time to time until it had emerged as something greater than reality? Was there any truth whatever in the tattered, stained pages of that document?

Superstition went back much further than religion; back to primeval man watching the lightning flash across the heavens and the deep voice of the thunder rolling back from the hills. Standing at the window, he looked out at the rounded hump of Cranston's Hill on the skyline and wondered.

* * *

The revelations of the manuscript must have entered his mind and affected his dreams for as he slept there came to him the most apocalyptic visions. He was out on the north road from Tormount, walking slowly in the direction of Cranston's Hill, feet dragging as though fighting against something that was urging him on. There was the feel of someone moving behind him, coming up to overtake him.

The other drew level with him and in the pale light he saw that it was Malcolm, yet this was not the face of the brother he had known. The grinning mask was evil and the grip on his arm, hard and tight, was one that could not be shaken off. In his dream, he was led towards that great mound and in the flooding light of a moon he could not see the hard angles of the Standing Stones stood out above him like a nightmare painting by Dali.

There were other presences too that he could sense, moving along with them and all the while, he was acutely aware of a distant, muted throbbing which seemed to soak through every pore in his body, a penetrating force that hinted at things more potent than mere sound. The familiar things which he had seen that morning now assumed in his dream the most unfamiliar and perturbing combinations. There was a suggestion of a vast stone set in the circle of tall columns, of hideous, blasphemous shapes that cavorted and leapt just at the edge of his vision. Then Malcolm released his grip on his arm, thrust something into his right hand and stepped away.

Looking down, he saw the white shape laid across the altar before him and beyond, the most demoniacal features his dreaming mind could conceive, staring into his while at the same time, an emanation of pure, unadulterated evil flooded around him.

There was the feel of something outside of him, struggling to enter his body, to take over his entire being. His right arm lifted of its own volition and the pale light glimmered off naked steel.

In his nightmare, the paralysis of utter fear seemed to hold him rigid for a terrible moment while all the time, his mind screamed at him that this was not real. His body was straining itself for flight, striving to tear itself from the grasp of terror. The deep throbbing in his mind went on and on. Voices seemed now to be murmuring, now to be shrieking, at him. The rest of the dream was monstrous and shadowy. In the nightmare he knew that he screamed out aloud, that somehow the terrible spell which held him in its grip loosened and he had turned from that dreadful place, was running back down the hillside, among those oddly-shaped growths and stunted trees while terror rode the wind at his back.

With a start, he woke, his body jerking spasmodically in the bed, his limbs bathed in sweat. Thrusting himself upright, he tried to slow the frenzied palpitations of his heart, telling himself it had been nothing more than a remarkably vivid nightmare brought on by reading that manuscript so soon before coming to bed.

Outside, there was a pale greyness in the sky. The dawn was already brightening. Stiffly he rubbed the muscles of his right arm where they had become cramped, then stared with a sharp sense of horror at the object clutched tightly in his fingers, his whole hand numb with the effort he had been exerting, Shocked, he dropped it on to the floor beside the bed.

He knew with a sick certainty, that he had left the knife he had found on Cranston's Hill in the study the previous evening. How then had it come to be clenched so tightly in his fist?

Shakily, he swung his legs to the floor, then stopped, staring at the mud spattered on the carpet and caked on his bare feet!

4

The Dark God Hunters

'The only possible explanation is that you must have been walking in your sleep,' Anne Cowdrey tried to suppress a shudder. 'A nightmare. And that house would give anyone the creeps.'

'I've never walked in my sleep in my life.' Amberley's voice was light but his face was deadly serious. 'No. There's something more to it than that. Something connected with that knife I found.'

'I don't understand.' Anne rose to her feet, brought more coffee. 'You mean that is what might have happened to Malcolm although in a slightly different way?'

'It's more than likely.'

'But how can a simple object like that still possess something which can affect us today?' she protested.

'It's stretching coincidence a lot further,' he told her. 'I'm positive that

Malcolm was driven to his death. So far, the only links I can find between the way in which he died and my own experience last night are that he was investigating these bizarre happenings on Cranston's Hill and he had the same kind of knife as that which I found.

'I think my next step is to have a word with Lady Parrish. She may be able to tell me something about the ancient history of the manor. There are one or two things which don't tie in with the old church records which the vicar lent me yesterday.'

'Would you like me to come with you?' Anne got up. 'Lady Parrish can be a little eccentric at times and she may not be quite as open with you as she would be if I came along.'

As they stepped outside, there was the crunch of footsteps on the gravel and a moment later, Doctor Cowdrey came along the drive. He gave Terence a friendly nod of greeting. 'Sorry I always seem to be out when you call, Terry,' he said warmly. 'I noticed you at the funeral — a tragic business that — but my former colleagues had bustled you off before I could have a word with you.'

'Of course, you retired from practice some time ago,' said Terence, remembering. 'It doesn't seem like five years since we last met.'

'Retired at the end of last year,' said the other. 'I still keep my hand in though with one or two of the older patients. They prefer me to Harmon. Don't know why and they refuse to accept the fact that I'm no longer the official doctor in the village. Still, Richard doesn't seem to mind and it gives me something to do in all of the spare time I seem to have now.'

It was on the tip of Amberley's tongue to ask the other if he knew of the weird occurrences that surrounded Malcolm's death, but the other spoke before he could get the words out.

'I've just been in to see Miss Munderford — our post-mistress. You may remember her, Terry.'

The other nodded. He vaguely remembered a tiny woman, grey-haired, with a pair of rimless spectacles balanced somewhat precariously on the end of her nose, always associating her in his mind with the large bicycle that she kept propped outside the tiny post office in the main street.

'A strange case,' went on the other quietly. 'The last person in the world I would have considered to be highly imaginative. My guess is that someone was playing a practical joke on the poor woman. I told her she should have had a word with Sergeant Willingham about it, but she seems convinced it was no joke.' He hesitated, looked ill at ease.

'What was it?' Amberley asked tightly. He had the odd feeling that he knew what Cowdrey was going to say.

'Apparently she had been visiting a niece of hers in Tenterton and stayed a little longer than she had expected. Since it was a clear night with some moonlight and she knew she had to be back in time to open the post office early this morning, she decided to cycle back. I don't suppose she would have done it normally. She's as superstitious as most of the others and you won't find any of these folk taking that road past Cranston's Hill after dark, except maybe for a few poachers out after rabbits or pheasant.

'Anyway, she had just 'cycled past the place and was maybe three-quarters of a mile from Tormount when she heard something in the fields to her left. She was in such a stew that she just put her head down and cycled as fast as she could.

'It seems that was the worst thing she could have done. The chain came off her bicycle at the bend and she wobbled into the ditch. Had she simply left it there and walked the rest of the way she may have got off with only a few scratches and bruises, but instead she tried to right the machine and slip the chain back into place.'

Terence could visualise the middle-aged woman struggling with her machine in the pale moonlight, out there in the wilds, with not a solitary soul around at that early hour of the morning.

Cowdrey scuffed his toe in the red gravel. 'What I'm going to tell you now doesn't make sense and if it had been anyone but Miss Munderford, I would have said they had been drinking. But I've known her all my life and she's a strict teetotaller. She claims that she had almost got the chain back on when she grew aware that there was someone coming down the road from the direction of the village. Naturally, her first thought was that here was someone who could give her some assistance and she got to her feet to move out into the middle of the road.

'How badly that spill had affected her, I don't know. But she claims that although she was certain it was a man in the road, there was something odd about the way in which he was moving that frightened her. He seemed to be *gliding* along rather than walking!'

'Perhaps it was just the moonlight playing tricks with her eyesight,' suggested Anne lightly. 'After all, she is extremely short-sighted.'

'No, she was adamant about what she saw. Then as the other came nearer to her, she saw who it was and she didn't wait any longer, forgot all about her cycle, and ran to the village as fast as she could.

She didn't stop running until she reached home and locked herself in.'

'But what could have — ' began Anne, surprised. Her father looked grimly at Amberley.

'She swears that it was your brother, Terence. She says it was Malcolm — or rather his ghost — she met on the road last night!'

There was silence for a moment, then Terence exploded: 'But that's impossible! Ridiculous. How could she have — '

'Don't ask me how it could have happened,' said the other, his tone suddenly weary. 'The only thing I am sure of is that it will be some time before she recovers from her experience. I gave her a sedative and she's sleeping soundly at the moment.' His eyes narrowed just a shade. 'I have the feeling that you think this may have something to do with the odd manner in which Malcolm died and those strange things he was investigating. You may think you can learn something by questioning her. If so, I'd like to ask you not to do so for a little while. Any excitement or mention of this could have a most serious effect on her.'

'Yes, I understand.' Terence gave a quick nod. 'As a matter of fact, Anne and I were on our way to have a talk with Lady Parrish. I was hoping she could give me some information on the manor.'

'She may.' The other suppressed a frown. 'You know, Terry, I can sympathise with you wanting to inquire further into your brother's death. But whatever you do, take my advice and don't go probing too deeply into these things. They are all best forgotten, I assure you.'

'Do you believe that Malcolm committed suicide?' Terence asked the other directly.

'I have to say — yes. I examined the body at Harmon's request and I do have some knowledge of his state of mind during those few weeks before it happened. He was in a highly nervous and excited state, and some of his actions were not those of a normal person. I'm sorry I have to say this, particularly at this moment, but — '

'I understand. Think nothing more of it,' said Terence warmly. He waited until the other had disappeared inside the house, then fell into step beside the girl. They passed through the wicker gate, latching it behind them and struck along the narrow lane that led obliquely from the main road to where the high gables of Tormount Manor showed among the tall beeches.

★   ★   ★

The long, gloomy hall of the manor seemed vaguely familiar to Terence as he walked along it, the suits of armour ranged along either side and the long portraits hanging on the walls, shrouded in dark grey or brown draperies. It was, he reflected, more than fifteen years since he had been inside the manor and then he had looked at it with the eyes of youth. Now, on this cold, bright morning, it struck him forcibly how dark the place was compared with the bright, healthy sunlight outside. It was impossible to tell how old the building was, except that it was certainly several centuries old, and there were perhaps only parts of it that dated back to the old times when the de Grinleys had first come to Tormount, before the evil terror of witchcraft had come like a dark plague.

The butler knocked on one of the doors at the end of the hall, paused for a moment, then opened it and stood on one side as they entered. The door was closed quietly behind them. This was a room Terence had never been in before, a bright, spacious room, clearly designed for being lived in. Lady Parrish rose from her chair as they entered and extended her hand, giving Anne a smile of welcome.

'I'm very pleased to meet you, Mr. Amberley,' she said. Her handclasp was firm for a woman. 'It must be a great many years since we last met.'

'Indeed it is, Lady Parrish,' Terence said, sitting down in the chair she indicated. 'Fifteen years or more.'

'But then it was under very different circumstances,' she murmured softly, leaning back in her chair. 'You'll take coffee, of course.'

'Thank you.' Terence nodded as she

reached for the bell pull. 'I hope we are not intruding, but there are some things about my brother's death which I don't understand at the moment and I was hoping you might be able to help me.'

'Naturally I'll do everything I can, but I don't see how — '

'Lady Parrish,' Terence began forcefully, 'I don't know whether you are aware of the fact, but apart from my brother, several people appear to have died in the village under mysterious circumstances, Malcolm's death being only the last of many. I've read through the old records from the church which the vicar kindly lent me and I'm convinced that there is something terribly evil here, something horrible centered on Cranston's Hill and also on the manor.'

Lady Parrish smiled faintly. 'I'm afraid you must be wrong about the manor, Mister Amberley. I've lived here for most of my life and surely if anyone should know if it were haunted, or anything like that, it would be me. But if you wish to look over the place, then you're quite at liberty to do so. I would show you around myself, but unfortunately my leg doesn't allow me to go scrambling around the cellars and the older wing as I used to.'

'May I ask just how old the manor is?'

'This wing dates back to the early part of the seventeenth century but there are some far older remains and I believe that the foundations go all the way back to the twelfth century. There was a lot of rebuilding during the latter part of the Middle Ages. You know, of course, that the manor originally belonged to the family of the de Grinleys. There are a lot of tombs in the vaults beneath the east wing but if you should think of exploring down there I would advise you to be extremely careful, That wing is now in ruins and unsafe in places.'

'We'll be very careful, Lady Parrish,' said Anne. She glanced at Terence. 'I used to go there exploring when I was a little girl.'

*　*　*

The older part of the house was, Terence reflected, evidently of the kind to attract the curious. He and Anne had moved out into the garden for there was clearly no connecting link between the modern living quarters and the far more ancient structure, which was, as Lady Parrish had said, falling into ruin. Even in the wintry sunlight however, Terence experienced a faint chill as he paused at the tumbled masonry of the entrance. There was about the place an odd and indefinable atmosphere of menace that touched the hairs on the back of his neck.

An air of tremendous antiquity lay over the shattered blocks of stone and the shadows held a midnight quality that intruded upon his mind as he paused and glanced about him.

'It does look a little creepy, doesn't it?' Anne said. Her voice, although soft, seemed to carry for a long distance, echoes bouncing off the looming walls and along the narrow, low-roofed passages that stretched away in front of them, seeming to lead down into the bowels of the earth.

'I don't blame her ladyship for staying away from the place,' he muttered. He moved deeper into the ruins with the girl following close behind. The stones underfoot were slippery with a sickly greenish mould and here and there, oddly shaped growths thrust themselves from the walls where the water trickled down the rough stone in tiny, glistening streams. All around them there was the stench of rottenness and decay, noxious odours rising from unguessable depths and long ages of time.

The sense of utter malignancy in that still, unmoving air was almost more than he could bear. The girl too was affected in the same manner, yet she managed to give him a tight little smile as they moved on. The enshrouding passage continued for perhaps fifty feet and then opened out into a wider chamber, pillared by tall stone columns. There were tiny slits in the stone that let in a little of the outside light but for the most part, the entire chamber lay in deep shadow. A faint scurrying in one corner caused him to jerk his head round sharply. There was a fragmentary glimpse of glaring red eyes and then a dark shape that skittered across the mouldy stone floor and vanished into another corner.

'Only a rat,' he said harshly as the girl started. 'Nothing to be afraid of.'

'I'm not really scared,' she said, 'just startled. I'd forgotten about them. This place must be full of rats.'

Terence advanced into the middle of the large chamber, dug into his pocket and brought out his lighter. He flicked it, held it over his head. The faint yellow glow did little to pierce the enveloping gloom. The distant corners remained as black as ever and as he stood there, he had the uncanny feeling that there were other things hidden there besides the mice and rats. God, what a place!

Cautiously, he edged his way forward an inch at a time, moving more by sense of touch than sight, with the girl holding on to his sleeve as though afraid to release her hold.

Here, even more than around the entrance, the long cracks in the solid stone were filled by whitish, fungoid growths, sickly and pale, which had never seen the light of day and as his eyes grew more accustomed to the gloom he noticed that ranged around the walls were long, wooden boxes whose contents he did not dare to imagine. Was this the original manor, built long before the modern building?

What he saw there forced him to the inevitable conclusion that it was, that this was part of the family vault of the terrible de Grinley line.

'There's a door of some kind over there,' Anne murmured. She pointed a trembling finger. 'I seem to recall that it leads down further into the foundations.'

'Are you game to go on?'

'If you are.'

The door, at the far side of the chamber was of stout wood, crossed by bands of iron, most of them rusted away, the wood splintered here and there, and warped by long ages of dampness. Through the cracks in the wood, a rush of foetid air flickered the flame of the lighter as he held it close, hinting at something more beyond.

Handing the lighter to the girl, he set his fingers around the edge and pulled with all of his strength. The door gave abruptly with a leaden, swinging motion. The blast of air brought a rush of nausea to his stomach and the light threatened to go out as the girl stepped instinctively to one side. Ahead of them, there was only a deep, almost material blackness.

With an effort, Terence forced himself to relax. What was there to be afraid of in this place? A few rats and the bones of the long-dead de Grinleys in those coffins along the walls behind him. Yet he still hesitated to go forward. The light from his pocket lighter only just illuminated the gleaming stone steps at his feet, steps that led still deeper into the ground, descending to unknown regions far below them.

Hesitantly, he stepped forward, feeling with his feet for the narrow steps carved from the solid stone. Anne clung tightly to his arm as they descended into the abysmal darkness. The pale, flickering glow of the lighter revealed the carvings on the walls of the narrow passage and halfway down, he paused, thrusting the lighter against the dripping wall to examine them more closely.

Anne shuddered. 'Who on earth could have carved such monstrosities?'

Time had effaced the images to a large extent, but there was still enough of them to be discernable. Utterly diabolical, they stood out in relief; nightmare demons from some hell known only to the artist and yet there was a curious familiarity about them that tugged at some hidden memory in Terence's mind.

Slowly, they descended further into the black chasm, down a haunted tunnel that rang with the muffled echoes of their footsteps. Once, as they neared the bottom, he thought he heard a faint sound from somewhere below them, a dull slithering which sent a spasm of sudden terror through him as he stopped, motioning the girl to remain silent. But there was nothing to be heard but the harsh sound of their own breathing.

'How much further does this tunnel go?'

Anne's voice reached him from the gloom. 'Not much further. We seem to have gone deeper than I remember it.'

Less than five seconds later, without any warning, the yellow glow vanished abruptly.

They had entered a wide vault far below the ground and there seemed to be a faint mist rising all about them, oozing out of the ground underfoot, glimmering a little around the tiny flame. Taking a couple of faltering steps forward, he realised that the floor of the vault was now level but the utter blackness remained impenetrable.

Then, something did become visible, looming out of the darkness to one side. He heard the girl's sharp intake of breath as she caught a glimpse of it and the clutch of her fingers on his arm tightened perceptibly.

Edging forward, holding the lighter out at arm's length, he strained his vision in a desperate attempt to make out what it was. Not until they had approached it to within a couple of feet was it recognizable. Oblong, perhaps twelve feet in length and half as much broad. It had been hewn out of a single block of stone with indications of the same horrific carvings around the base. There were vague inscriptions too and Terence bent forward in an attempt to decipher them, but the writing was in no language he knew. He straightened up abruptly, the lighter almost falling from his shaking fingers.

'I think I know what this is,' he whispered. 'It's that altar which used to stand on top of Cranston's Hill, among the Standing Stones. It must have been removed and brought down here centuries ago.'

A niggling feeling at the back of his mind struggled to assert itself. Long centuries must have elapsed since this great stone altar of Belial had been brought down into these stygian depths and the hands which had performed that stupendous task had been dead for hundreds of years, could no longer harm them. Yet why had it been removed from its original position among the Standing Stones? Why had anyone gone to such trouble to move it? The bulk and weight of the thing must have made it an almost impossible task. God alone knew how they had succeeded in shifting it.

'Let's get out of here,' he said hoarsely. 'I think we've found what we came for.'

Together, they felt their way back to the slippery flight of steps. A feeling of something evil seeped around them, oozing from the walls and the floor. Not until they were out in the open, among the weeds that grew huge and thickly around the tumbled ruins, was he able to calm himself down sufficiently to reason things out logically.

'I never want to go down there again,' Anne said, white-faced. 'All those coffins along the walls. Were they — '

'The entire line of the de Grinleys,' he nodded. 'Except of course, Richard de Grinley, the last of the line.'

'You think there could be any truth in that old tale? That he never did die?'

'I've been through the records carefully and there's no mention of his death anywhere, but that doesn't really prove anything. And apart from opening those coffins and — '

'Don't, Terry,' said the other sharply.

She placed her hand on his arm. 'Let's go back to Lady Parrish, but let's not tell her anything of what we discovered down there. It would only upset her and she's an old woman now.'

* * *

That evening, as Terence sat at a late meal, the ringing of the doorbell interrupted him. He rose sharply, walked swiftly along the hall and opened the door. Treherne stood there with Doctor Harmon close behind him.

'Mind if we come in and have a little talk with you, Terry?' said Treherne. 'It could be a matter of life and death.'

Terence led the way to his study. Inwardly, he felt oddly disturbed by this visit. Both men looked extremely grim.

Harmon seated himself in the chair by the fire, stretching his hands out to the blaze. 'I want you to stop these wild investigations of yours,' he said bluntly. 'I understand from several of the villagers that you've been wandering around in the ruins of the old manor.'

111

Terence felt a quick stab of anger pass through him. 'I presume you have some reason for saying this, Doctor?'

The other nodded his head curtly. 'This is exactly how your brother acted during the months before he died. There was naturally a lot of antagonism against him on the part of the villagers. Since his death, they began to feel that all of this was over and forgotten. Now you've started raking it all up again they don't like it.'

Terence shrugged. 'I'm afraid I fail to see what business it is of anyone what I do. I'm not satisfied that my brother committed suicide. Nothing is going to prevent me from finding out the truth of what really happened.'

Treherne leaned forward. 'No doubt you are doing this with the best of intentions, Terry, but the repercussions as far as you are concerned could be quite serious.'

'I don't take kindly to threats, Ralph.'

Harmon took a slim folder from his inside pocket, spread it out on his knee. 'This is the full report on Malcolm

Amberley's death. You may read it if you wish.'

Terence made no effort to take the report.

Harmon folded the papers and thrust them angrily into his pocket once more. 'Then I take it that you won't stop this unwarranted questioning and prying into other people's affairs?'

'That's right. Since I've been here I've discovered things that convince me that whatever it was my brother was investigating, it was far more than a mere legend. That weird experience in the churchyard when Malcolm was being buried.' He shot a quick glance at Treherne, saw the other's face change. 'You saw it too, Ralph. You saw that — thing — standing there among the trees. You were scared out of your wits then; and you still are.'

'There was nothing there but the mist and the trees.'

'Then why were you shaking so much you could scarcely stand? Perhaps whatever evil exists up there on the top of Cranston's Hill came down into the

113

churchyard just to make certain he was dead.'

'Don't say anything like that!' Treherne said in a harsh whisper. 'You meddling fool, Terry! You don't know what you're doing — '

'Take it easy, Ralph.' Harmon gripped the other's wrist tightly. 'We've done our best by warning him. If he refuses to heed that warning then the consequences will be on his own head.'

He got to his feet, helped Treherne to his. As they reached the door at the end of the hall, Treherne turned to Terence. 'Your brother was my friend, Terry. I tried to warn him — and now he's dead. For God's sake, take warning before the same thing happens to you.'

Terence said nothing, watched as the two men left and walked out into the lane. Just before they vanished from sight behind the tall hedge, he had the unmistakable impression that they were having a heated argument. Then they were gone. He closed the door and went back inside.

The tea on the table was cold. He went

over to the small cocktail cabinet and took out the bottle of whisky that Malcolm had evidently bought and only half drunk. He poured himself a stiff drink, carried it back to the fire.

Just what had those two in mind, he wondered? What possible concern could it be of theirs? Were they afraid that he might bring unwanted publicity to this isolated backwater of a village if news of this should leak out? Or was Harmon afraid of his reputation as a doctor if he did discover that Malcolm had not committed suicide?

He sipped the whisky slowly, feeling it bring some of the warmth back into his chilled body. God, but it was getting cold! Finishing his drink, he got to his feet, checked the windows for any draught that might explain the strange coldness in the room. There was nothing.

Going out into the hall, he made his way slowly up the stairs. His fingers closed around the handle of the door to his room when something attracted his attention to the door at the far end of the passage. It was not one of the rooms he had examined and he had no idea what lay beyond that closed door.

He sensed that this seeping wave of numbing coldness came from within that room, emanated there and swept down to blanket the whole house.

On sudden impulse, he went to the offending door, twisted the handle sharply, half-expecting it to be locked. But it opened easily under his touch and he peered inside, trying to make out details in the faint shaft of light that spilled in from the corridor. The room seemed empty, totally devoid of furniture. He fumbled along the wall just inside the doorway, searching for the light switch, but found nothing.

Pushing open the door, he went inside. The room seemed curiously lighter than he had expected, almost as if there were moonlight filtering into it, yet there was no window, or if there was, some heavy curtains had been drawn over it.

Shivering a little, he went further inside. His elbow brushed against something hard and he gave an involuntary cry, staggered back a couple of paces, then saw that it was a tall metal candlestick. At least he could have some light by which to see. Taking out his lighter — which he'd refilled on returning to the house — he lit the candle, the wick spluttering a little before it finally caught.

Suddenly, everything in the room sprang into clarity. Sudden revulsion swept through him. There were no carpets on the floor of this particular room but instead there were odd cabalistic designs in glaring reds and blues; a five-pointed star, at each point of which was a small cup of clear crystal, curiously fashioned and half filled with a pale green, nauseous-smelling liquid. Something like terror settled on him at the sight but that which was still to come unnerved him completely.

In his ears there came a low, distant throbbing, a muted humming which changed continuously in pitch as though voices were muttering in muffled tones a great distance away and at the same time his nostrils were stung, revolted, by the shocking stench which rose up in the room like an invisible, noxious vapour.

Automatically, he began to back away

towards the door.

Before he had taken two shambling paces across the bare floor, something incredibly evil and malignant seized him so that it was impossible for him to move. He stared as if hypnotised at the centre of the floor, the oddly bare patch between the points of the pentacle. Somehow, he seemed to have known the moment he entered the room that there was evil here, but even he was not prepared for the horror that met his wide-eyed gaze at that moment,

Out of the floor there steamed and bubbled a putrescent vapourous swirling of mist, a sickish, almost luminous fog which thickened as it hung in the pale candlelight and seemed to develop strange and oddly shocking suggestions of form and shape. The overpowering thrust of hate and malevolence enveloped him, blighting his senses until he would have staggered and fallen to the floor had not this demoniac force held him rigid and unmoving. Shadowy and monstrous, it reared up until it towered above him and now he saw that it had definite shape.

There were the outlines of a leering face, of glaring eyes filled with unbridled cruelty and devilish intent. This was the Devil incarnate, supernatural evil that passed beyond all human comprehension. There was no way of fighting it. He could feel himself being drawn irresistibly forward, his feet dragging reluctantly as he attempted to call upon every nerve and fibre of his being to resist.

What terribly potent powers it drew upon, he did not know; nor why it had come. Clearly those terrible designs had been made to call this thing from whatever realms beyond human knowledge it came. Desperately, he tried to tear his gaze from that terrible face, the pointed chin and drooling mouth, the low, slanting forehead topped by two four-inch horns. It was no good.

He felt himself falling forward into a bottomless well of utter blackness.

Unable to help himself, feet shuffling forward like a drunken man he moved closer to that demoniac spectacle. The arms reached out for him, the tremendous force exuded by that blasphemous abomination pressing on his chest until it felt as though he could no longer breathe and his heart threatened to stop its frenzied beating.

When something splintered with a tinkle of broken glass beneath his foot, there was a simultaneous surge of sound inside his skull; a wild, echoing shriek of rage and savage pain that clove through the mists shrouding his brain.

There was a swirling of mist before his stultified vision, a cloying, sickly smell as of an opened grave and then slowly, painfully, reeling from the terror and exertion of the experience, he fell back against the wall, his knees buckling beneath him as he sank to the floor.

Gradually, his eyes focused. In the middle of the pentacle, a tiny thread of the liquid from the smashed cup oozed across the dusty floor.

5

The Haunted and the Damned

Amberley's condition was, for long moments, one of indescribable chaos. Not knowing whether he was sleeping or awake, whether he was mad or sane, he somehow pushed himself up on to his knees, staring fixedly at that thin trickle of liquid on the floor.

Somehow, he struggled to his feet. The spluttering candle flame flickered as he brushed past it, was extinguished as he reached the door and burst out into the corridor, half running towards his own room. The bolt on the inside slid home with a rasping of metal on metal and it was not until then that he managed to relax a little.

He did not undress, but sat for a while on the edge of the bed near the window, waiting for his heart to stop pounding. The sheen of perspiration on his forehead felt cold and clammy to the touch. At that moment, he was not willing to say whether what he had witnessed was a nightmarish hallucination or a hideous fact. The lingering stench tended to confirm that it had been real, that what he had seen in that terrible room was one of those blasphemous monstrosities spoken of in the old records and hinted at by generations down the long centuries. Such fiendish designs as those on the floor were said to possess strange properties and no doubt Malcolm had known of this from those weird books in his library.

This legacy of an insane legend which had haunted Tormount for more than five centuries might well have acted on the minds and imaginations of the people who lived there, bringing a form of contagious madness to them all, with only a few exceptions and now it was affecting him to the same extent. Who could be sure of what was reality and what was nightmare after reading those hideous tales written on the documents that the Reverend Ventnor had given him, documents he kept under lock and key for fear of what they might do to imaginative men? Was it at all possible that this latest occurrence was simply delusion, some form of self-hypnosis?

He stretched himself out on the bed, in his ears the moan of the wind around the time-weathered eaves.

Closing his eyes, he tried to sleep, but drowsiness did not come. In the distance, he heard the faint chime of the distant clock in the church steeple as it struck the half hour. Turning over on to his side he fixed his gaze on the pale square of the window where the moon was just beginning to come into view behind the slow-moving clouds that obscured it at intervals. He found that he was subconsciously listening for something, a sound which he dreaded but to which he could put no name. The church clock chimed the hour of three. Still there was no other sound but the groans of the ancient woodwork and gradually a fatigue settled over him so that in a little while he dozed off into a dreamless sleep.

It was grey dawn when he woke, his body stiff and uncomfortable. Swinging his feet to the floor, he got up. What he had been through that night was now highly uncertain in his mind; yet he felt that there was something unutterably hideous in the background.

Was this what Treherne had been trying to warn him about? The fact that this aura of evil that lay over the village could, at times, when the signs were right, materialise into something more than mere legend?

He stayed in his room for the best part of an hour before shaving and going downstairs, deliberately averting his gaze from the half-open door of the room at the far end of the corridor. He ate a hurried breakfast, was on the point of carrying the dishes through into the kitchen when there came a knock at the front door.

'Good morning, Terry.' Anne gave him a bright smile, stepped past him into the hall. She noticed the dishes on the table, turned. 'I came over early to cook you some breakfast. It occurred to me that you might not be eating well, having to fend for yourself. It seems I'm too late.'

'I didn't sleep very well last night,' he said defensively. 'I got up early and cooked something for myself.'

Her brows drew together. 'Something wrong, Terry? You look as if you'd just seen a ghost.' Her smile faded as the implications behind her words struck home. Hesitantly, she added: 'You haven't, have you? Seen a ghost, I mean.'

It was on the tip of his tongue to relate to her what he had seen, or had thought he had seen in that room at the top of the stairs. He decided against such a course. There was no point in frightening her any more than was absolutely necessary.

He shook his head slowly. 'I spent too much time reading those curious books of Malcolm's before I went to bed. And I had some harsh words with two of the village's most respected citizens.'

'Oh?' She looked up from the cup of coffee she had just poured for herself.

He forced a faint grin. 'Doc Harmon and Ralph Treherne came to see me last night. They were very insistent that I should stop prying around in the village. They were certain it would be dangerous if I continued, that I would end up the same way as Malcolm did.'

He saw her eyes cloud a little. 'And will you stop?'

'Not now. I can't. I'm beginning to convince myself that Malcolm was on the track of something diabolically evil, which will have to be rooted out and destroyed. What happened six or seven hundred years ago in Tormount must have been so terrible that the evil associated with it still persists. There are some scientists who believe that both good and evil emanations can cause vibrations in the ether which live on long after their originators are dead and forgotten.'

'I wonder why Treherne and the doctor were so anxious for you to give up,' mused the girl. 'Now that you mention it. Doctor Harmon tried to dissuade Malcolm, almost to the point of threatening him.'

'Either Harmon is afraid of losing his reputation as a doctor, or there is a deeper meaning for all of this. It may be that — ' He broke off at a sudden rattle on the front door letterbox.

Anne smiled. 'You've got mail.'

He rose quickly to his feet. 'I can't imagine anyone writing me here — unless someone in London wants to see me urgently, although that doesn't seem likely.'

He came back holding a small envelope. 'I don't recognize the writing.'

'Perhaps if you opened it, you might find out who it's from!'

He nodded absently, slit the envelope and took out a single sheet letter. The address as the top was a street in Nottingham, but he did not take much note of this until later. It was the letter itself that mystified him.

It was brief and to the point:

'Dear Sir,

I understand you are investigating certain happenings in and around Tormount. It is imperative you see me as soon as possible. This could be a matter of life and death.'

He handed it to the girl without a word. The look on her face as she read through it was a blend of surprise and bafflement. 'Who on earth is Clivedon

127

Park?' she asked, staring at the signature at the end of the letter. 'Do you know him at all?'

'I've never heard of him,' Terence said truthfully. 'Unless he was some acquaintance of Malcolm's, although he never mentioned the name to me. It certainly isn't one you would forget easily once you heard it.'

'What do you think it means? A matter of life and death. Perhaps he's just another crank, some dabbler in the occult.'

'That's more than likely. On the other hand, it is just conceivable that he may have some important information.'

'Then you're going to see him?'

'Yes.' He glanced at his watch. 'It's only eight-thirty now. I could be in Nottingham in less than an hour.'

'May I come with you? This is getting more interesting every day.'

'Somehow,' Terence said grimly, 'I have the feeling that it will turn out to be far more dangerous than interesting.' He thought of that fiendish thing he had seen in the room upstairs and felt on the point of refusing to take her with him. Then it came to him that perhaps she would be safer with him in Nottingham, rather than alone in the village.

'All right. I'll get the car ready and meet you in the main street in fifteen minutes.'

★ ★ ★

A gentle daylight rain misted the air as they drove through the outer suburbs of Nottingham an hour later. Fortunately, Anne knew her way around the city and the street they were seeking, not far from the banks of the Trent, was easy to find. It was a narrow, winding street, unlike the broad thoroughfares through the centre of Nottingham and as he stopped the car outside the small house, set back from the road behind a thick hedge, Terence had the feeling that here, time had passed by leaving little evidence of its passage.

There was no sign of life as they rang the bell and waited, but a few moments later the door opened on faintly creaking hinges. The figure that stood there was that of an elderly woman, tall and stiff as a ramrod with a tight bun of grey hair on the back of her head. She looked at them inquiringly in silence so that Terence was forced to speak first.

He held out the letter. 'I received this from a Mister Park,' he said pleasantly. 'He asked me to call and see him as soon as possible. My name is Terence Amberley.'

'Oh yes.' The woman nodded stiffly. 'Mister Park told me to expect you. Please come inside.'

Lowering his head as he passed beneath the low lintel, Terence followed the other into the narrow, dingy hallway. It was difficult to know what he had been expecting, but certainly nothing like this. The walls were decorated with hideous death masks and over one door at the end, a white skull grinned eyelessly at them as the woman rapped on the door with her knuckles and called loudly:

'The visitor you expected is here, Mr. Park.'

There was an unintelligible bark of sound from beyond the door but the woman evidently understood for she thrust it open and motioned them inside. The man who stood at the narrow window, his back to them, must have been well over six feet tall, but his stooped posture made him seem much smaller. He was as thin as a rake, the jacket much too short for him so that the almost skeletal wrists showed bonily at the ends of the sleeves.

As he swung abruptly to face them Anne found it difficult to suppress a sudden cry of surprise. The sharply-angled features were dominated by the unruly thatch of white hair and the piercing, gimlet eyes which stared from Terence to Anne and then back again. The bushy brows lifted for a moment in an unspoken question.

Terence said quickly, 'This is a friend of mine, Mister Park. Anne Cowdrey. She is helping me in my investigations at Tormount.'

'I see.' For a moment the lips parted in a mirthless smile. 'I wonder if she will be as anxious to help you when she has heard all I have to say.'

'I beg your pardon?'

The other lifted his right hand. 'Please sit down, both of you. I will have Mrs. Forsyth bring us some tea and biscuits. You will have had a long journey here.'

Terence glanced at the girl, then sat down in one of the hard, high-backed chairs. He peered around the gloomy room. The window was very narrow, the gloom accentuated by the thick curtains, drawn so that only the barest slit of daylight filtered in. Almost as if the other was afraid of the daylight. The conviction came to him that his initial supposition had been correct. Mr. Clivedon Park was nothing more than a crank, someone who dabbled in these esoteric mysteries and tried to set himself up as an authority on the subject. He probably did a little card-reading and performed at local amateur séances in his spare time.

The door behind him opened. Clivedon Park said: 'Some tea and biscuits for my guests, please.'

'Very good, Mr. Park.' The door closed as quietly as it had opened.

Terence held out the letter towards the other. 'I'm not sure that I understand this. I gather you have some information you want to give me and that you consider it important.'

'Important!' exclaimed Park harshly. His eyes positively gleamed beneath the thick brows. 'Important! I wonder if you know just what forces you are meddling with, Mr. Amberley?'

Moving towards them, he sat down at the small table. 'It is quite evident to me that you don't. That is why I asked you to come and see me, before something terrible happens — to both of you.'

'Then you know something of what is going on there?' interrupted Anne.

'Exactly, Miss Cowdrey.' His gaze switched towards Terence. 'Your brother was extremely interested in the legends associated with Cranston's Hill and the surrounding countryside near Tormount.' He ran a finger down the long, pinched nose. 'Oh, we never met. You won't have heard of me from him. But I know more of what he was doing than you realise. I read the coroner's report of his death. Suicide they said, didn't they?'

'That's correct,' Terence said dully.

'Blundering fools!' exploded the other. 'Imbeciles! Whenever they come across anything they cannot understand, they have to cover it up with meaningless words, and then proceed to forget about it all. I don't blame the coroner. He could only find a verdict on the evidence that was presented to him. It's those bureaucratic fools who provided him with that evidence and withheld the rest simply because it did not fit in neatly with what they believed happened, that I blame. When we are face to face with evil, we cannot escape it by running away and saying that it does not exist.'

'Then how — ?' Terence broke off as the door opened again and the housekeeper came in with the tray.

She set it down on the table beside Clivedon Park, made to pour it out, but he waved her brusquely away. Waiting until the door had closed behind her, he said sharply, 'How can we possibly fight it? That depends on a great many things. There are ways, but the danger is extremely great and the price of failure exceedingly terrible.'

'You mean that we might die as Malcolm did?' asked Anne in a hushed whisper.

Clivedon Park stared at her intensely for a long moment. 'I mean that death would be the easiest thing to face. There are things in this world — and out of it — which are more terrible than death.'

Terence felt the chill begin to gather in his chest once more. He realised at that moment that his original opinion of this man was wrong. Here was no charlatan. Here was a man who knew what he was talking about.

'I see that you get my meaning, Mr. Amberley.' The other's voice was calm and even. 'But I am forgetting myself as host.' He poured out the tea pushed the plate of biscuits across to them.

Terence sipped the hot tea slowly, then said: 'What exactly is your interest in this business, Mr. Park? You evidently know a great deal about what has been happening yet I fail utterly to see why it should worry you what happens to us.'

'But of course, how stupid of me. There is no magic in the fact that I know so much. As you will have guessed my interest in the occult began many years ago. At first, like you, I was a complete sceptic. A crowd of hysterical villagers see something on top of a lonely hill with a very dubious reputation and immediately there is talk of a Satanic Mass being held up there and within a century or so it has grown into a veritable legend. A man draws some of the ancient symbols on a bare floor, mutters a handful of unintelligible phrases found in some handbook of magic and a demon appears. Self-induced hypnotism. Mere superstition. The annals of the Middle Ages are full of such reports.

'More than forty years ago, I decided to devote my life to examining these old legends, to try to find the tiny grain of truth which might lie at the back of them all. I persevered, and as time went on, it was soon evident to me that amid this morass of lies and half-truths, there were cases that could not be satisfactorily explained. Now I know that these things did exist, still do exist. Evil can be a very potent and dangerous force, Mr. Amberley. Just as we believe that miracles have been performed in the past when the force of good became sufficiently strong to over-come the normal natural laws by which we are governed, so the force of evil can also be evoked to carry out deeds of destruction.'

'And this aura of evil which exists around Tormount is just such a force?'

'Undeniably. That is why it is extremely dangerous for anyone who does not understand it to meddle. You know, of course, about the de Grinley family?'

'Yes. They appear to be involved in this legend.'

'More than that,' insisted the other, leaning forward in his chair. 'Richard de Grinley is the basis and the truth of it all.'

'I don't understand,' murmured Anne. 'In spite of what the records say, or rather what they didn't say, he must have died more than four hundred years ago.'

'Maybe the creature that called itself Richard de Grinley died all those centuries ago,' said Clivedon Park softly, 'but not the devil that was in him.' Clivedon Park got swiftly to his feet. 'You are aware, I suppose, that people died in

137

large numbers in Tormount during the sixteenth and seventeenth centuries.'

'Burned or hanged as witches and warlocks, you mean?'

'Not at all. Oh, that went on, there's no doubt about it. But there were others found behind locked doors with terrible marks on their bodies, lacerations and bruises that could not be satisfactorily explained. The records will show that they died of fright — but in locked rooms with no entry or exit for anything material?'

Terence finished his tea, sat back in his chair. 'All this is very interesting, Mr. Park. And we certainly appreciate your warnings. But they make me only more determined to get to the bottom of this affair.'

'I never thought otherwise,' answered the other promptly. 'All I ask is that you allow me to help you. To be quite honest, I've waited more than twenty years for a case such as this.' There was an almost childish eagerness in his tone. 'In case you are wondering how I came to know all of this, perhaps I should explain that I have a kindred spirit in Tormount who has kept me up to date with these odd occurrences, including certain aspects of your brother's death which, in all probability, you know nothing about.'

Terence nodded slowly as the realisation came to him. 'The vicar.'

'Quite right. The Reverend James Ventnor. He telephoned me early yesterday, said that he had given you certain documents. I gather you still have them.'

'I have them safely locked away,' Terence answered. 'Even to me, it was quite evident that they should not be seen by normal people.'

'In short, you are now beginning to believe that the whole array of facts which we have at our disposal point to some lingering influence still existing over Tormount?'

'Let's simply say that I intend to keep an open mind on the subject,' Terence said. 'But as for your offer to help. I would appreciate it greatly. So far, my knowledge of the supernatural has been confined to what little I've read on the subject and — '

Clivedon Park had been standing

before the narrow window. Now he swung round sharply, hands clasped tightly behind his back. 'Are you quite sure of that, Mr. Amberley? You've had no contact with these forces on a more material plane?'

'There was that odd experience you had a couple of nights ago, Terry,' said Anne before he could confirm or deny what the other had said.

'Ah, now we may be getting somewhere.' Excitement tinged the other's voice. He lowered himself back into his chair, eyes gleaming ferally. 'And what was that?'

For a moment, Terence found himself off balance. 'I suppose I must have been sleep-walking. It's a perfectly natural explanation.'

'Perhaps. But let me be the judge of that. Go on.'

'Very well. I had found an old knife on top of Cranston's Hill, evidently of great age and very similar to that which they found in my brother's body. I took it back with me and as far as I can recall, I locked it away in the desk before reading through those records that the vicar lent me. That night I had some kind of nightmare. I can only recall a little of it but it seemed as though Malcolm led me to some kind of meeting on top of Cranston's Hill. I do remember standing over some altar with someone lying on top of it, and Malcolm thrusting that knife, or one like it, into my hand. It was as if I was being ordered to sacrifice that victim on the altar and yes, there was something more . . . ' he could not repress the shudder at the hideous memory. 'Some horrible creature standing opposite me on the far side of the altar, some thing that did not even look like a man.'

'What then?' commanded the other sharply, as he paused.

'Nothing very much. I must have woken at that moment. But the odd thing was that when I woke I had that knife clutched in my hand and there was dried mud on my bare feet and on the floor of my room.'

'So.' The other ran a horny finger down his cheek. 'There's little doubt in my mind that this was more than a mere case of sleep walking as you seem to think.' He took a quick turn about the room, head bowed forward even more than normal.

Finally, he ceased his restless pacing, drew himself up to his full height.

'I think I shall return to Tormount with you, Mr. Amberley,' he said forcefully. 'I know that my good friend, the vicar, will put me up for a few days and I would certainly feel far easier in my mind if I were on the spot so to speak. There are certain aspects of this case which worry me intensely.'

'By all means.' Terence glanced sideways at Anne. She was smiling faintly. Perhaps she considered Clivedon Park to be merely a strange and eccentric dabbler in the occult, who could not really be of help. Maybe she was right, he reflected, as they waited for the other to give instructions to the housekeeper. But there could surely be no harm in indulging the other's whims, strange as they might appear.

★ ★ ★

Half an hour later, they were driving through the early December sunshine, the bare fields stretching away on either side of them, the crowded city streets left far behind. Out here, in the bright sunlight, all of those dark terrors that he had recently experienced seemed to have faded into relative insignificance. Maybe it was the presence of Clivedon Park in the back seat who had suddenly brought things back into a more normal plane by his oddly cartoon-like manner and appearance.

They drove through a small village set on the slope of a hill, the gabled houses set back from the road, everything looking peaceful and normal. Yet as they topped the rise, there were glimpses of the dark, primal forest in the distance, dense and mysterious and in spite of the sunlight it was not difficult to imagine how it must have been some five centuries before when this was the witch country of England.

Clivedon Park suddenly stirred in the back seat. 'One thing I would like to ask, Mr. Amberley. When I last visited

Tormount, about ten months ago, I was introduced to your brother. He was then living in the old house at the end of the lane. Might I inquire whether you are now living there?'

'Yes, I thought it better to move in rather than inflict myself on Treherne. Besides, I had the feeling that I might find some clue as to what really happened in the house.'

'I see.' Park ruminated for a moment, then: 'I suppose you've seen that room on the top floor, the one at the far end of the passage?'

Terence's fingers clenched convulsively around the wheel. Then he nodded. 'I discovered it last night. Why do you ask?'

'Never mind that now.' Park sat back in his seat. 'Just answer me one question. Did you notice anything strange, unusual, when you were in that room?'

When Terence remained silent, the other went on slowly: 'I thought so. Something did happen last night that you haven't told me about. If I'm to help you, you must tell me everything.' His voice was rising a little in pitch now. 'What was

144

it? A sensation of heat? Cold? You didn't — ' He paused significantly. 'You didn't see any material manifestation of any kind?'

Terence half turned to reply, then swung back and concentrated on his driving. His mind was a turmoil of half-formed thoughts and ideas. He knew that Anne was watching him closely a puzzled frown on her face. 'All right,' he muttered finally. 'I did think I saw something in that room. But looking back on it, I'm sure I must have imagined it all.'

'You never told me anything about this, Terry,' Anne said, her tone sharp.

'I didn't want to worry you with my wild imaginings,' he said weakly.

'Perhaps you'd better tell me — *now*!' said Clivedon Park's voice from the back seat. There was an odd note of authority in it.

'Very well. Although it sounds so insane I doubt if you'll believe me.' Briefly, he related to the other what had occurred.

Clivedon Park remained silent until he had finished. Then: 'You had an extremely lucky escape,' he said gravely. 'Extremely lucky. I never guessed that your brother had progressed so far. He must somehow have translated some of the old writings.

'Fear has lurked around Tormount for more centuries than anyone can remember. For many years that stone-topped hill has been the centre of wild stories. Monstrously hideous stories of a lurking evil that can sometimes take a kind of human form, but only so long as there has been a recent victim in the village or the surrounding countryside. I'm afraid we shall have to fear the worst now.'

'What do you mean?' asked Anne in a frightened whisper. She turned in her seat to stare at him.

'Simply this, Miss Cowdrey. If the old records are true, then whatever this evil is, it becomes dormant after a certain length of time, becomes half forgotten except in the wild tales the villagers whisper among themselves. But now and again, someone comes along who pries into these things more deeply than the others, goes through with some of the ancient rites — calls up these terrible monstrosities if you like — and inevitably falls victim to them. When that happens, this evil force is released, renewed a thousand-fold to ravage and destroy. Your brother, Mr. Amberley, was just such a person. Now he's dead and once again, this eldritch fear is loose around Tormount. That thing you saw last night was no figment of your imagination. Would to God that it was!'

His voice trailed off into an uneasy silence that persisted all the way through Tenterton and into Tormount. In the early afternoon sunlight, the village slumbered peacefully in the valley but as they drove towards it, Amberley had the uneasy feeling that this was only a surface tranquility.

He stopped the car outside the rambling vicarage sitting beside the ancient church with its ivy-clad tower lifting towards the blue, unclouded heavens. The Reverend Ventnor was in the garden as they drove up. He straightened from his pruning of one of the bushes glanced round and then came towards the gate, wiping his hands on a piece of rag.

He showed little surprise at seeing Park. Shaking the other by the hand, he said genially. 'I expected you to come down sometime. You seem to have a nose for these things.'

Clivedon Park nodded, but there was little amusement on his thin, cadaverous features. 'From what our friend has been telling me, I seem to have come just in the nick of time,' he said gravely.

6

The Satanists

There was thunder muttering over the surrounding hills two nights later; a storm that had blown up suddenly from the north-east, dark, scurrying clouds blotting out the stars which had been clearly visible only half an hour before. Inside the front room of the rectory there was a pleasant warmth from the fire crackling in the hearth and a similar glow in Terence Amberley's stomach from the two whiskeys he had drunk.

In front of the fire, the vicar drew on his heavy overcoat buttoning it with fingers that fumbled a little in his nervousness.

He said throatily: 'You're quite sure that you want to go through with this, Amberley? It isn't too late, even now, to change your mind. This is something so highly unprecedented that I doubt if I should really be a party to it, certainly not without a court order and a direct command from my bishop.'

'I can understand your feelings, my dear Ventnor.' It was Clivedon Park who spoke, his long length stretched out in one of the chairs. 'Believe me, if I thought there was any other way of proving to ourselves the full extent of what we are up against, I would be the first to consider it. Unfortunately, there appears to be no other way.' He shot Terence a piercing glance. 'We must exhume your brother's body. I realise that we are breaking the law, that if you, or the vicar here, should decide to lift that telephone and 'phone the authorities, then I could be jailed for quite a long term.' He heaved himself upright. 'But somehow, I don't think you would do that. With Ventnor along with us there will be no question of sacrilege.'

Outside, the rain slashed against the windows with a sudden fury. It was certainly not the sort of night for a nocturnal mission such as this, Terence thought soberly. The three of them had talked this matter over all afternoon until they were dry of talk. At first, the thought had horrified him and he had been against the idea completely; but Clivedon Park had eventually succeeded in persuading him that what they were fighting was far stronger and far more evil than anything he had ever conceived and that the act of exhuming his brother's body was a minor matter compared with the consequences of what would happen in the inevitable course of events if he refused.

'Just what do you expect to find, Park?' Ventnor asked thinly. 'As you're well aware, I've been following events in the parish for some time now, ever since I first suspected what might be happening. I even put some of my doubts and fears before the bishop but I'm afraid he is a very practical man and refuses to believe anything of this sort without some concrete evidence. Something that, unfortunately, I did not have.'

'That is exactly what I am hoping to provide you both with tonight,' declared Clivedon Park vehemently. 'I assure you I wouldn't dream of doing this for any other reason.' He gave a wry smile. 'The conception of a material form of evil is one which few people will take seriously these days. The progress of science seems to have relegated everything like that to the airy realms of mere superstition. Only a select few of us know the terrible and diabolical forms which evil can take. Search back through the history of the parish, Ventnor. See how many of your predecessors attempted to exorcise this place of evil and how often they failed utterly and miserably.'

Ventnor rubbed his hands together nervously. 'I agree.' he murmured finally. 'But even if we do find what you suspect, how do you propose that we fight this evil when so many dedicated and good churchmen failed?'

'That, I'm afraid,' said the other, 'is a bridge we shall have to cross when, and if, we come to it. For the moment, I am simply attempting to obtain facts. Until we know where we stand, we can scarcely be expected to make plans, beyond protecting ourselves with some fundamental precautions.'

'You mean this,' Terence said. He opened the neck of his coat and pulled out the large silver crucifix, which Ventnor had given him earlier.

'Exactly. That is one of our protections. The cross has long been one of the greatest forces against evil. Even before the beginnings of Christianity it was used by the ancient priests of various cults, developed from the still earlier charm in the form of the swastika.'

Terence replaced the crucifix, buttoned up his coat. He glanced at his watch. It was a little after eleven o'clock. 'All right then. What are we waiting for? Let's get this thing over with as soon as possible.'

Stepping outside, closing the heavy door of the rectory behind them, they staggered as the full force of the wind struck them like a physical thing. Rain slashed and hammered at their bowed faces. Clivedon Park, in addition to the heavy spade, carried a closed lantern, while Terence held a powerful torch in his left hand, swinging the beam ahead of him as he followed the others along the path which led through the rear of the garden and into the grounds of the nearby church.

The rain soaked him to the skin within moments, his overcoat flapping around his legs as he walked, leaning forward into the wind. There was a demoniac voice in the wild shriek of it as it screeched through the clawing branches of the trees, rattling the boughs over their heads with twitching fingers. Underfoot, the ground was a morass of mud and puddles that gleamed fitfully in the light of the torch and lantern.

His mind kept returning to that odd question which had been troubling him ever since this nightmare had begun; and again he wondered what fiendish method Malcolm could possibly have used to call up this evil entity, this — could it possibly be a reincarnation of Richard de Grinley — which now seemed, if Clivedon Park could be believed, to have brought the terror back to Tormount with a vengeance.

There came a vivid thunderbolt of lightning to the north and lifting his head instinctively, he saw, before the light had temporarily blinded him, the great, rounded summit of Cranston's Hill, standing out on the skyline, crowned with those tall stone columns. The titanic roll of thunder, bursting almost directly overhead, deafened him and he cringed involuntarily, blinking the rain out of his eyes.

There was a sharp click as the vicar unbolted the gate in the hedge. On either side, the trees dripped mournfully, shaking down huge drops of water on to their heads. Baleful trees of a tremendous size and age, their trunks warped and twisted by the long centuries, leered down at them as they passed through and into the churchyard. In the near distance, the massive bulk of the church itself loomed up before them. The square tower showed briefly in a wall of grey as more lightning flashed across the berserk heavens. This time the thunder which followed seemed a little further away, almost as if the storm were retreating somewhat. But he knew from past experience that thunderstorms in this part of the country could continue for hours, moving around the hills on all sides, hills that seemed to attract the lightning and thunder.

Beyond the line of scarred trunks in the foreground, illumined by the lightning, rose the grey headstones, some half obscured by trailing creepers and the dark patches of moss that had overgrown them. Ventnor paused a moment later, looked about him as Park held the lantern high over his head, then pointed wordlessly.

'That way,' he shouted, raising his voice to make himself heard above the whine of the wind. 'I'll lead the way.'

Feet slipping in the mud, they progressed in single file, scarcely able to lift their heads as the rain struck with a million fingers at their eyes, half blinding them. Moving around one corner of the church they were sheltered from the full force of the storm for a few moments and Terence sucked deep gusts of air into his straining lungs, pausing to wipe the rain from his eyes. Park turned and looked back at him. 'No time to back out now Amberley,' he called. 'We've got to go through with it.'

'I'm not backing out,' he gasped. 'Just trying to get my breath back.'

'Good. I thought for a moment you were beginning to have doubts.' The other seemed satisfied. 'I agree this isn't the sort of night for doing this sort of thing, but it suits our purpose. I'm anxious that none of the other villagers should know what we're doing. On any other night, there might have been someone watching.'

'You think they'd try to stop us?'

'I'm convinced they would,' said the other enigmatically. 'But not, perhaps, for the reason you think.' He turned and followed the vicar, his coat tails flapping in the wind and rain like some monstrous vampire strutting among the headstones.

Terence pulled himself together, shuffled after the two men, along a narrow, twisting path that led to the far corner of the churchyard. Here, Ventnor paused to get his bearing, then moved off a couple of yards and pointed down at his feet.

'This is the one,' he said confidently. 'But what has happened to all of the wreaths which were placed here?' He waved an expressive arm to indicate the scattered mass of crushed flowers, leaves and stems. 'Who could possibly have done this?'

Park placed the lantern on the sodden ground, then straightened, holding the spade in both hands. 'The important question is,' he said tightly, 'not who did it, but why it was done.' Without waiting for any reply, he gripped the long handle of the spade tightly in his hands and plunged it into the soft earth.

* * *

Maybe something has happened to me and I'm getting callous about all this, thought Terence to himself. They had been digging for almost twenty minutes and now, as he straightened his back with an effort, he saw by the pale glow of the lantern that the hole was more than six feet in depth. It was just possible to see Park's head and shoulders whenever he straightened to throw a spade of dirt on to the heap beside the grave.

The thunder was still muttering away in the distance but now it was several miles away and the flashes of accompanying lightning few and far between. The rain still fell in sheets but the wind had died appreciably and it no longer slammed against them like an unleashed animal in the darkness. The night air was bitterly cold however, and he felt numbed in every limb.

When Park's spade struck something more solid than earth, the hollow thud sounded abnormally loud in the quietness. In spite of himself, Terence started violently.

Clivedon Park's head appeared above the edge of the hole a moment later. 'This is it,' he said hoarsely. 'Hand me down the lantern.'

Terence handed the other the lantern. The faint yellow glow faded a little as the other lowered it into the hole with him and the smooth walls of moist earth gleamed as the light was reflected off them. Now they could see nothing of the other beyond the monstrously magnified shadow that moved on the earthen walls. With an effort, Terence resisted the urge to step forward and peer down. At that moment, it was all he could do to prevent himself from turning on his heel and running from that place as fast as his legs would carry him.

Why, in God's name, had he agreed to this terrible thing? Whatever happened, he fervently hoped that Anne never got to hear of this; for somehow he doubted if she would ever understand their reasons. Muffled sounds came from below and then, after what seemed an eternity, he heard Park's sudden exclamation.

Ventnor started visibly. 'In heaven's name, what is it man?'

Park's head appeared once more. He held the lantern in his hand and placed it carefully on the ground near the mound of earth. In a voice that was not quite steady, he said: 'I think you had both better take a look at this. Shine that torch of yours down here, Amberley.'

Switching on the torch, Terence edged forward, shone the powerful beam down into the hole. The beam wavered violently in his unsteady hand. Then it finally steadied. As it did so, he felt the blood rush from his face, felt the cold chill of superstitious awe and fear settle on him.

This was madness! Utterly insane!

In the torchlight, they were able to see the splintered lid of the coffin where it had evidently been smashed by some tremendous force. *But the coffin itself was empty!*

Ventnor was muttering something under his breath but it was impossible for Terence to make out the words He stepped back as Clivedon Park placed his hands on the ground and hauled himself up. A moment later, the other was standing beside him.

'Help me to fill it in again,' said the other sharply. 'There's clearly nothing more we can do here. This has merely confirmed my worst fears.'

The rest was shadowy and vague. Terence worked like an automaton, not pausing until the job was finished.

Not until they were back inside the rectory did his mind begin to work again, more under the warming influence of the large glass of brandy which the vicar had poured out for each of them, than from any active direction of his own will.

'What on earth could have happened,'

the vicar was the first to find his voice. 'I mean — what we saw there. Why should anyone do a thing like that?'

'Remember that we were on the point of doing it,' put in Clivedon Park tautly. He ran his fingers through his sparse hair. 'The question is, where is the body now?'

Terence leaned forward, startled. 'Can we be sure that Malcolm really is dead?' he asked tightly. 'Maybe this is some hoax being played on us. Maybe he never was in that coffin at all.'

Clivedon Park shook his head. 'I realise just how much you would like to believe that your brother is still alive. Unfortunately, everything points to the very opposite.'

'Go on.'

'You saw for yourself that the coffin in the grave was empty. There was, however, one thing you did not see. When I uncovered the coffin, the top was already smashed, splintered almost as we saw it.'

'Then someone must have opened it some time in the past three or four days,' said Ventnor.

'Someone did,' affirmed the other

soberly. 'But this was not a deliberate act of vandalism as you may think. You see — the coffin lid was smashed open from the *inside*!'

'Oh God!' The vicar's sharp exclamation sounded unnaturally loud in the still room.

★　★　★

There was no sleep for Terence Amberley that night. Instead, he sat in the chair by his window struggling to arrange his almost incoherent thoughts. There was evil here, evil that seemed to come seeping in a black, nameless tide from the rounded summit of Cranston's Hill, flooding from that terrible, blasted space among the Standing Stones.

Getting nervously to his feet, he put out the light and moved close to the window in the darkness. The village, that part of it he could see, was in almost total darkness.

The only light that showed came from a window in the rectory and he guessed that neither the vicar, nor Clivedon Park,

163

would be asleep. Were they trying to make plans in the light of what they had now discovered? Would the three of them be strong enough to face up to the danger when it came? Was there any way at all by which they could overcome it?

He stood there for several minutes, eyes scanning the dimness outside. The pale sickle of the moon now showed low on the eastern horizon. The storm had gone, but it had not cleared the air; rather it seemed sultrier than before. Sweat trickled in rivulets down his back.

Somewhere, a faint humming seemed to have started up, faint and strange and so far away he could not be sure that he really was hearing it at all. There were sounds that maybe only the mind hears and not the ears. Just as a dog can pick up the shrill, silent blast of a note pitched too high for human ears, so this seemed to be entering his skull through the bones.

He turned his head slowly, trying desperately to discover the source of the sound: but it seemed to be coming from all round, muttering through the air, focusing itself on his receptive brain.

At times, it would retreat into the distance, before burgeoning up into a throbbing hum that quivered through his limbs as if a million tiny electric shocks were being discharged through his flesh.

He stood quite still, rigid, near the window. Then, of its own volition, his body began to move towards the door. It was as if an unseen hand had caught him by the arm and was propelling him forward, unable to help himself.

Perspiration ran into his eyes, yet he scarcely felt it. There was only those terrible fingers of evil power catching hold of his mind, directing him to he knew not where.

His oddly numb fingers twisted the handle, forced open the door. Like an automaton, he moved down the stairs, into the study at the front of the house.

Through the mists that enveloped his mind, Amberley struggled mentally to resist, but to no avail. The throbbing beat in his head grew louder, more insistent and demanding. There was no fighting it. This, thought a tiny part of his mind, was what Treherne and Harmon had warned him against. Yet how could they possibly have known about this evil power?

Utterly in the power of this terrible mental force, he unlocked the drawer of the desk, reached in with nerveless fingers and took out the ancient sacrificial knife.

There was a sort of diabolical crackling in the air of the room, a crackling which he knew could exist only inside his own head. Something was drawing him on now, out of the house.

The chill air closed about him. The haziness in his mind grew deeper and yet with that tiny part of his mind which still remained to him, he was acutely aware of all that was happening, could feel the wind on his exposed face and head and it was then that he noticed something.

Although most of the houses in the village were in total darkness, there was a pale glow flickering at the very edge of his vision.

He jerked his head round with a puppet-like motion until he was staring straight at it and the horror came flooding through him as he saw where it originated. In the distance, a mile or so away, the tall, rearing columns of the Standing Stones stood out in stark silhouette against the shimmering red glow of hell-light that shone on top of Cranston's Hill touching the undersides of the lowering clouds with a glow like that from the Pit itself.

The utter malignancy of that glow awakened the most frightful fancies. With slow, jerky movements his body moved along the lane, his unwilling feet continuing to carry him forward. The vast thunder of the sound filled his head like some great drum beating between the grey walls of his skull.

He sensed that everything he had done, everything that had happened since he had arrived in Tormount, had been designed to bring him out on this very night.

Reaching the end of the lane, where it linked up with the main road through the village, his feet sloshing through the puddles, he paused as if unsure in which direction to go. There was an unholy hush over everything. It was not the silence that came from a village in which every inhabitant was asleep; rather it was that of a place which had been long abandoned.

Turning, facing towards that hellish glow on the horizon, he began to shuffle forward. This was surely the end. He could no longer help himself: he was completely and utterly in the grip of something diabolical and satanic.

A low branch caught him in the face as he staggered to one side. Automatically, he put up a hand to it. There was blood on his fingers where long thorns had torn his flesh but no pain.

Vaguely, he was aware of what seemed like voices but they were almost drowned by the sound inside his head and he could not tell from which direction they came, or even if he was only imagining them.

Something struck him on the back. Half falling, he threw out his hands to save himself, went down on one knee. Then there was the feel of something being thrown around his neck. For a moment, he struggled. It was as if there was a fire burning in his chest, a boring agony that seemed to pierce him through to the heart. The next instant, almost before he was aware of it, the spell was broken. His mind was abruptly clear.

A searing pain across his forehead told him where the thorns had scratched deep into his flesh. His head rolled loosely to one side and the breath came harsh in his throat, gasping through his tightly clenched teeth.

Dimly, he was aware of the tall, almost skeletal figure that loomed over him, the other's face bent forward until it almost touched his, a face that gleamed in the moonlight, the white hair like a halo around the head. The eyes, he noticed, were dark and piercing, were now filled with a look of concern.

'Are you all right, Amberley?' Clivedon Park was yelling the words at him.

For a moment, resentment welled up inside him, then subsided quickly as he staggered to his feet, the other's arm helping him up. Another arm came round to support him about the waist and turning his head stupidly, he saw the vicar peering up at him, a look of horror and fear on his broad, chubby features.

'I think I'm all right.' Somehow, he managed to get the words past his trembling lips. 'What happened? How did I get here?' He realised he was shivering convulsively, violently.

His fingers touched something cold and metallic against his chest and he stared down in surprise. The silver crucifix had been tossed around his neck and now hung down in front of his shirt, gleaming brightly in the moonlight. So that was it!

'I hope I didn't hurt you too much,' said Park harshly. 'But in the circumstances there was nothing else I could do. Another few moments and it might have been too late.'

'We shouted when we saw you, but you didn't seem to hear us,' explained the vicar. 'You were like a man in a trance.'

'That's exactly what he was,' boomed Clivedon Park. Taking Terence's arm, he led him back along the road towards the village. 'Why in God's name did you take off that crucifix?'

'I — I don't remember doing it.' He fumbled with the buttons of his shirt. 'I guess I must have done it automatically when I got in.'

'It was a damnfool thing to do,' muttered the other. 'Still, you probably didn't realise the full implications it could have. You'll know better the next time.'

As they reached the end of the lane, Terence turned to look back to the northern horizon. The glow that he had seen on top of Cranston's Hill was no longer there. Maybe he had only imagined it, after all. He shuddered in his wet clothing.

'Tell me,' he mumbled weakly, 'did it really happen? There seemed to be a peculiar vibration in the air and then something got hold of me, forcing me to leave the house.'

'Yes, it happened all right. This wasn't a dream. Now, at least, we know something of what we're fighting here. We were watching from the window of the rectory and fortunately, the vicar spotted you moving along the lane. It's as well that he did, otherwise there is not a thing we could possibly have done for you if they had got you out to that accursed place yonder.'

Terence allowed the others to lead him

back to the house. There was still a light showing in the hall. Closing the door behind him, the vicar went into the living room, poked the dying fire briskly until it blazed up again, then piled further logs on to it, holding his hands out to it as the sparks danced up the chimney.

'I think we should remain here for the night,' said Park grimly. 'There is always the possibility that they may try again. We may have won a skirmish, but this isn't the whole battle. That is still to come.'

Sinking into a chair, Terence lay back. The pain in his forehead had now subsided to a dull ache. Putting up a hand he touched the long scratch gingerly with his fingers. The blood was beginning to congeal on the wound.

'I've never had any experience like that before in my life,' he muttered.

Clivedon Park drained his glass, set it down on the nearby table. 'One of the faculties often attributed to witches and warlocks in the Middle Ages, was the power to call their victim across great distances. It still happens in Africa. They call it talking to the bones out there, I believe.'

'It just doesn't seem possible.'

'I assure you that it is. We're dealing with dark and powerful forces here. But already the pattern is becoming clearer. The village was virtually empty. There was no sign of life and I think I know why. *They were all up there on Cranston's Hill!*'

7

The Shadow Over Tormount

Terence Amberley stared at Park in stunned disbelief. Then he turned to look at the chubby face of the vicar, who nodded in answer to his unspoken question.

'I half-suspected it some time ago,' he said harshly. 'While your brother was still alive, there were nights like this. I used to stand at my window and look out over the village. Not a single light showing anywhere, except maybe over at the Cowdreys.'

Terence felt a small sense of relief at this. The idea that Anne might be mixed up in this terrible evil was almost more than he had dared face. Now, at least, it seemed that this was not the case. Besides, he told himself fiercely, she would scarcely have gone down into those frightful vaults beneath the old manor if she was in league with them.

At length, he found his voice. 'But why do they do it? Surely there has to be a reason why people like this, so normal and pleasant during the daytime, change at night.'

'It's an old story,' began Clivedon Park softly. 'Go back through the ancient records and you will find periods when the village was seized by this strange form of madness. In those days they were content co call it witchcraft — black magic — and today, is there a better name we can give to it? You saw how easily this power could affect your mind, force you to do things against your will. Only the power of the crucifix prevented you from joining them up yonder. They have no such protection.' He rose to his feet. 'Now that we are here, perhaps you could show me this room upstairs.' There was no mirth in his thin-lipped smile as he added: 'If they do try again tonight, that is where the danger will come.'

As they reached the top of the stairs, Park laid a hand on his arm and motioned him to silence. For perhaps two minutes they stood there, listening for any sign that there was anything out of the ordinary up there. Park gave a brief nod of satisfaction. 'Let us go on,' he whispered softly.

Slowly and carefully Terence turned the handle and opened the door. Halting on the threshold, he stepped to one side as Park went in ahead of him. There was a brief pause, then the scrape of a match and a moment later a flare of yellow light as the other found and lit the tall candle just inside the doorway.

Dreading what he might see, he went in with the vicar close on his heels. But the room was empty. There was none of that terrible chill which he had noticed on the last occasion and this gave him a sense of relief. At least, if that coldness was associated with the evil when it came, they might have a little warning, time to get out.

The stain on the floor, where the liquid he had spilled had dried in the dust, was clearly visible. Park stood close to the weird design and looked about him carefully. The expression on his face and the tense posture of his tall, thin body reminded Terence of a hunting dog at bay, searching out some prey.

Terence had the unshakable feeling that eyes were watching them from the dark corners where the dancing yellow glow from the flickering candle did not seem able to penetrate.

He turned his glance back to the strange symbols drawn on the floor at his feet, aware that the vicar was doing likewise.

The longer he looked, the more the scene fascinated him, and he somehow sensed a potent source of evil residing in the mathematical suggestion of the strange designs. The pointed star and the circles all hinted of some remote time, of half-forgotten secrets from unguessed at abysses of centuries and the monotonous repetition of the figures was sinister in the extreme. He found himself thinking too of those strange images he had seen in vague outline on the walls of the vaults deep below the foundations of the old manor, every contour of which seemed overflowing with the ultimate quintessence of unknown and potent evil.

He jumped visibly as Park spoke again. 'Your brother must have delved far more deeply into these things if he was the one who drew these designs. He must have been crazy to think he could control the forces he released.'

'I'm still wondering why he should have done such a thing,' put in the Reverend Ventnor. 'Surely no one in their right mind would call up things such as this.'

'I'm not passing judgment on him,' grumbled Park in his rumbling voice. 'I'm merely trying to find the most logical explanation. People go in for black magic for a variety of reasons. Some are simply looking for some form of excitement, others have prayed to God for some wish near to their heart and when it has not been granted to them, they inevitably turn to the devil. Some do it out of sheer curiosity and yet more because they are searching for power and believe that this way they may obtain it. Too often, the power they seek turns on them and destroys them utterly.'

'I only wish I could help you as far as

Malcolm was concerned, but we were never very close and during the last few years we lost contact with each other. I heard from him occasionally, but he never mentioned any of this.' Terence waved an arm expressively to embrace the clashing colours on the floor of the room.

Clivedon Park smiled wryly. 'It is hardly the sort of thing one would confide to another,' he remarked.

He moved over to the far corner of the room, began poking around on a narrow shelf which Terence had not noticed before, a low shelf set close against the wall.

'Take a look at these,' Park said after a moment. He motioned them forward.

There were several books reposing on the shelf, many looking as if they were on the point of crumbling into dust.

Some were bound in what seemed to be shiny leather, the pages curling and yellow-stained, the cryptic writing virtually indecipherable in places.

'Priceless,' murmured Park; 'Utterly priceless. How on earth he managed to get hold of these I'll never know. Good

God, some of these books have been considered lost for centuries and this one here — ' he picked one out held it up to the light — 'has been considered merely a myth by many seekers in the occult. I can see now where he got the knowledge to draw those symbols on the floor and the incantations necessary to raise these terrible powers.'

'I think I know where he may have found them,' Terence spoke almost without thinking, driven by some deep conviction within himself. 'In the vaults beneath the old manor. I went there the other day.'

The Reverend Ventnor looked round in sudden surprise. 'Vaults! Under the manor? This is the first I've heard of them.'

'Anne Cowdrey was with me at the time. We went along to see Lady Parrish, to ask about the manor. I thought that perhaps there was something there, which would give me a clue about the work Malcolm was doing, before he died. She told us that the present building dates back only a couple of hundred years or so, that the old manor was situated some distance away. Anne remembered playing there when she was a girl, down in the vaults under the ruins.'

'And you went down there?' said Park with a trace of excitement. 'Tell me, were there any signs that the place had been used as a family vault at one time?'

'If you mean were there any coffins there, then the answer is yes. Obviously it was the burial place of the de Grinley family. They're ranged along the walls of the first vault.'

'The first vault,' repeated Park. 'Now this is extremely interesting. Was there anything else?'

'Only one thing. At the bottom of the steps, there's an even larger underground chamber, completely empty as far as we could tell in the darkness, except for a large stone altar in the very centre. I think it must be the — '

'The Altar of Belial. Taken from the middle of the Standing Stones,' interrupted Park breathlessly. 'So that's where it went. The most obvious place in the whole village and therefore the last place anyone would think of looking.'

'I think that Malcolm went looking there and I think he probably found it, and it's my guess that he also found those books down there — unless they were among the other records locked away in the church vestry, Vicar.'

Ventnor shook his head decisively. 'I've never seen them before,' he confirmed. 'You must be right.'

Terence's eyes rested on the books for some long seconds and there was a nagging, growing uneasiness in his mind,

Park said suddenly: 'I think we must go along and take a look at this subterranean chamber, Amberley. But not tonight, of course. Maybe you could take us sometime tomorrow?' The bushy brows lifted in twin, wide arches over the keen, blue eyes. 'I have a hunch,' he added dryly, 'I hope it's wrong, but I have a very nasty feeling it may prove to be right.'

★   ★   ★

In spite of his firm intention not to sleep that night, Terence dozed off in the high chair, with a blanket wrapped around his legs, the effect of the whisky negating any wakefulness there may have been in his mind. When he woke, he was cold and stiff and outside, the world was yawning greyly as the first flush of dawn showed over the distant hills.

Park was still awake, seated in one of the other chairs near the fire which he had obviously kept built up all night. He was poring over the pages of one of the books that he had brought back with him from that room upstairs. Ventnor however, was fast asleep, his head lolling over the edge of the chair opposite, his mouth open, his snoring the only sound in the room apart from the faint crackling of the blazing logs in the hearth.

Getting up, Terence stretched himself. Every bone in his body ached and the sleep had not refreshed him. He felt curiously drained of life and energy and his head ached badly. Gradually, his memory came back as he put a hand to his throbbing forehead; he winced as his fingers touched the long, bloody scratch there. Last night had been no dream.

'Feeling any better after your sleep?' inquired Park, looking up. He laid the book down on the nearby table. 'I thought it best to let you sleep on, after what you went through last night. Besides, we have a lot to do today, or had you forgotten?'

'About the vaults?' Terence shook his aching head. 'I hadn't forgotten. And I'm afraid that if anything I feel worse.'

'You'll be all right once you get some food into you. Where's your kitchen? I'll make us something to eat.' He held up his right hand as Terence made to protest. 'No, I'm really quite a good cook. Even my housekeeper would accede to that. Just you sit down and take things easy. And I'd wash that cut on your head if I were you and get some disinfectant on it. Some of these thorn scratches can be quite nasty if you neglect them.'

Terence could think of no answer to that and while the other busied himself in the kitchen, he washed and shaved, feeling a little better. The cut on his forehead had bled a lot, but it looked worse than it actually was. By the time he had finished, the other had returned.

'Better give our friend a shake or he's liable to sleep all day,' said Park, nodding towards the inert figure of the vicar.

Ventnor came awake instantly at Terence's touch on his shoulder, starting up sharply. Then he relaxed a little as he stared about him. 'I've cooked us some breakfast,' Clivedon Park told him. 'Better eat it while it's hot.'

The meal was eaten in silence, each man engrossed in his own private thoughts. By the time it was over, the sun had come up and it promised to be a fine, bright day with the wind blowing from the south,

Half an hour later, they left the house, walked briskly along the lane and into the village. Pausing in the middle of the main street, Terence found himself seeing things through new eyes. On the surface, nothing was changed. Everyone was going about their daily work as though they did not have a single care in the world. As he watched them, listened to their cheery greeting to the vicar and himself, he found it impossible to believe that Park could have been right in his supposition that these common, ordinary people had left the village the previous night and had gone up to the top of Cranston's Hill for some diabolical purpose.

He found himself watching their faces closely, particularly their eyes. It was said that one could tell a man's thoughts by the expression in his eyes. There was the impression that they did give him a curiously furtive look whenever they thought he was not watching them.

'I must go to the rectory and let my housekeeper know that I'm quite safe,' said Ventnor. 'She will be wondering what on earth has happened to me when she comes in and finds that my bed has not been slept in.'

As the other had prophesied, they found the housekeeper, a little woman in her late fifties, was extremely agitated. She was clearly relieved to see the vicar safe and sound as they entered.

'So there you are, Reverend,' she said hurriedly, She spoke with the nervous eagerness of one who is eager to please. 'I called you when I let myself in half an hour ago, and when there was no answer and I saw that your bed was still made up, I was just on the point of going along to Sergeant Willingham to see if he knew anything about your whereabouts.'

'Now there's absolutely nothing to be worried about, Mrs. Weston,' soothed the other gently. 'I'm quite all right as you can see. I went over to visit Mister Amberley last evening rather late and decided to stay the night. I'm afraid we got to talking and it was well past one o'clock before I realised what the time was.'

'Have you had your breakfast? It won't take me five minutes to get it ready for you and — '

'There's no need to do that, Mrs. Weston. I had something to eat. Besides, I have to go out again very shortly. Some extremely important business has come up. I shall probably be out most of the morning.'

'Very good, sir.' The woman nodded, paused for a moment and then bustled away into the back of the house.

'A kindly soul,' murmured the vicar,

'but sometimes she can be a little too concerned about my welfare.'

'I was thinking that perhaps we should pay a call on Lady Parrish first of all,' Clivedon Park said. 'I presume that the manor is still her property.'

'Oh, certainly. Although she will raise no objection I'm sure. She rarely gets out these days. She had a serious illness some time ago, it affected the power of her legs She can manage about the house, but that's about the limit of her excursions these days. A great pity.' He shook his head a trifle sadly.

Less than fifteen minutes later, they were knocking on the door of the manor. Around them, in the garden the last of the red and yellow chrysanthemums were in bloom struggling to add what little colour they could to the general dreariness of the winter scene. A few late bees scorning the nip in the air, were humming among the flowers. Listening to them, it was difficult for Terence to imagine that there could possibly be any evil in this place.

Lady Parrish, the butler informed them,

would see them in a few minutes. In the meantime, would they please wait in the library? He showed them into the room at the back of the house where Terence and Anne had met her ladyship on the previous occasion. While they waited Park moved over to the wide French windows, peered out over the lawn where it sloped down to the line of trees at the bottom of the long garden.

'Are those the ruins you mentioned?' He pointed.

Terence went over and stood beside him, nodded. 'Yes, I believe it was once a wing of this house, but since it fell into decay it's been allowed to crumble.'

'The original home of the de Grinleys,' Park seemed to be speaking his thoughts aloud. 'It makes sense I suppose. Richard de Grinley must have known that sooner or later, the people would rise up against him and his evil masters, they would want to destroy everything associated with him. So he somehow took the precaution of having that altar removed and brought there.'

'But how on earth did he manage that,

unless he had several people to help him. You haven't seen the thing, but it must weigh more than a ton. Even in these days it would be a large enough engineering job and — '

Before he could finish the sentence, the door behind them opened and Lady Parrish came into the room, leaning heavily on her stick. She seemed a little surprised at seeing Terence there but smiled warmly and motioned them to sit down.

'I must apologise for not meeting you when you arrived, but apart from Anne Cowdrey who often comes over, I get so few visitors and I tend to sleep late in the mornings.'

'It is we who must apologise, madam,' said Clivedon Park. 'Unfortunately there are certain things which have happened in the village during the past few days which we feel must be looked into before they get completely out of hand.'

A look of puzzlement spread over her ladyship's features. 'I beg your pardon, but I'm afraid I don't understand. What sort of things?' She allowed her gaze to drift towards the vicar. 'Is it something to do with the church?'

'Only indirectly, I'm afraid,' murmured the other. 'May I introduce my friend, Clivedon Park. You might say that his — profession — is the very opposite of mine and yet in a way we are working towards the same end, the desire to see good triumph over evil. Whereas I am more concerned with the spiritual welfare of my parishioners, he pursues the same ends on a more — ah, materialistic level.'

'I still don't quite understand.'

'You may say that I'm a seeker after truth, your ladyship,' boomed Clivedon Park. 'I am more interested in the darker side of religion, the reality which lies behind the old legends of places such as this.'

The expression on Lady Parrish's face did not alter materially, yet Amberley felt certain that there was some slight change. Then the look was gone and it was impossible for him to be really sure that he had actually seen it. A look of fear at the back of her eyes, perhaps? A faint stirring of revulsion?

'Am I to understand that you believe, as Mr. Amberley does, that his brother's death on top of Cranston's Hill was not suicide?'

'I'm utterly convinced of it,' the other assured her. 'In fact, I would go further and say that it was some evil force which brought about his death. A force that is still active in the village, which could destroy everyone in Tormount unless we can put a stop to it, once and for all.'

'I'm sorry, but I can't believe that. It's too fantastic for words.' She turned her glance on Terence. 'I'm sorry if I have to say this in front of you, Mr. Amberley. I know how you must feel about the way your brother died, but you can't go in the face of the facts. They were all brought out at the inquest, so I'm told. As for this ridiculous suggestion of evil, what possible proof do you have?'

'Nothing that would stand up in the eyes of the law,' Park admitted. 'But more than enough to convince ourselves.'

'And why have you come to see me?'

'I think I can explain that, Lady Parrish,' said Terence. 'When Anne and I

192

came to see you a couple of days ago, we went down to the old manor. There are certain things in the vaults down there that may give us additional proof. What I saw down there scared me and I'm quite prepared to admit it. I'm no expert, but Park here has seen these things before, would know what was important and what was not.'

'And you want to go back there?'

'With your permission, of course,' said the vicar smoothly. 'Believe me, I would not be a party to this if I did not believe that there is something in what these two men say. I've seen things these past few days which I would never have admitted to be possible had I not witnessed them with my own eyes.'

Still Lady Parrish hesitated. Terence glanced at her in surprise. She had readily given Anne and himself permission to go through the old ruins. Was she afraid that whatever they might discover down there, it had the power to bring things to a head? Did she more than half suspect the grim and terrible truth that lay behind all of this?

Lady Parrish nodded reluctantly. 'Very well, Vicar. I suppose there is nothing I can do or say which will stop you from going through with this ridiculous notion you have. Although what it is you expect to find down there I can't imagine.'

*   *   *

After the torrential rain of the previous evening, the grass and moss-covered stones were still wet and treacherous and they were forced to pick their way carefully among the fallen blocks of masonry. One false move and it could have meant a broken limb at the bottom of the narrow passageway that led into the bowels of the earth. The vicar had taken the precaution of bringing a torch with him and he played the light over the dark, moisture-running steps as they made their way downward. All around them was a chaos of fallen blocks of stone and then the midnight black rift began to yawn, the stone walls here contrasting oddly with those above the ground. It was almost as if some other race had carved this great cavern that led beneath the massive foundations.

A faint, insidious stream of cold air trickled up from below, touching their faces with chill, clammy fingers. What primal, inconceivable force, what benighted devilment, had prompted anyone to build these subterranean vaults? Merely as a burial place for the de Grinleys? His mind rejected that notion, persisted in seeking some other reason for it.

He moved automatically after the tall, lanky form of Clivedon Park, with the tubby figure of the vicar bringing up the rear. More and more, he felt as if he were in the clutch of some compelling fate. The brilliant beam of the torch held in Park's hand provided far more light than had his lighter on that previous occasion and now it was possible to see in much clearer outline the hideous carvings which adorned the walls of the downward sloping passage. Park had seen them too, for at intervals, he paused in his descent and bent to examine them more closely, saying nothing, but nodding his head occasionally as though confirming that this was something he had expected to find.

The sinister incline continued for perhaps thirty feet and then levelled off into the first chamber, the vault of the de Grinleys. Park halted, swung the beam of the torch around the dank walls, overgrown here and there with the leprous white fungoid growths and patches of a greyish moss that bore an unwholesome and unhealthy sheen in the light.

'You were obviously right,' Park's voice echoed back to them, booming loudly off the enclosing walls. 'This is the burial vault, without a doubt. Did the church records have any mention of it, Vicar?'

'For most of the family the records are preserved in the church,' answered the other, striving to keep his voice down as if afraid of the mocking echoes. 'But they do not mention exactly where the burials took place.'

'No doubt they wanted that kept secret from the rest of the villagers,' said the other grimly. 'They must have had the foresight to realise that in those days of witch hunting, any relics might be destroyed by the mob.'

He walked slowly to the wall, bent to examine one of the coffins laid on the wide stone shelf. In places, the masonry seemed loose and unsafe and some bygone seepage of water into this region had worn a deep channel down one wall, leaving strange incrustations on the stone.

After a while, Park came back, cast the beam of the torch over the roof of the vault before advancing towards the far wall. 'I take it that the passage to the lower chamber is in this direction?'

'Yes.' Terence pointed. 'That way if I remember rightly.'

Reaching a convenient distance from the far wall, Park ran the beam of the torch over it. For a moment, it wavered indecisively, then steadied as it fell upon the rough-hewn opening in the stone. In spite of their brilliance, the rays of the torch shone only feebly into the engulfing blackness of that down-sloping passage. It cost Terence a tremendous effort to follow the others. He thought of that frightful chamber below them and again that sense of fate driving him on came vividly into his consciousness. He was acutely aware of the dampness, the chill cold and the moving flow of air that sighed up from the black depths.

Here, in the torchlight, the carvings were easy to trace at close range; and the complete, awful linearity stunned the imagination and conjured up visions of dark nightmare.

How long it took them to work their way down that terrible passage, it was impossible to estimate. Park heaved aside a piece of tumbled masonry at the bottom, then turned and flashed the torch on to the steps to guide them.

Cautiously, they advanced towards the centre of the chamber, the torchlight easily picking out the massive block of stone. Park walked around it slowly, flashing the light on it as he examined the inscriptions minutely At length, he straightened. There was a peculiar look on his face, the angular features etched with shadow.

'There's not the slightest doubt about it. This is the Altar of Belial. If I remember rightly, Richard de Grinley swore that he would never die so long as this remained within the confines of the parish. Everything is beginning to fit into place now.'

'I only wish I could understand it.' Terence said helplessly. 'What can we do?'

'You'll both have to trust me,' said Clivedon Park solemnly. 'First I want to copy some of these inscriptions down. Hold the torch for me, Vicar. Then tonight, we shall have to pay a visit to Cranston's Hill. I think it only fair to warn you that there will be considerable danger. You don't have to come with me unless you wish.'

'What kind of danger?' asked the vicar. 'Spiritual or physical?'

'Both,' Park had already gone down on one knee in the inch-deep dust, had pulled out a notepad and a pencil from his pocket and was busily copying down some of the ideographs which had been deeply carved around the base of the altar.

While he was engaged in this, Terence moved away from the others and acting on impulse, began to search around the walls of the vast chamber. Some instinct seemed to be driving him on. There were carvings here too, all blighted by the inevitable decay of centuries, In one corner, a tremendous mass of the vaulting had fallen and as he worked his way over it, clutching at the stone with his fingers, his hand encountered something small and metallic. Clasping it tightly, he carried it back to the others.

'You've found something?' The vicar glanced up as the other held out his hand towards the light.

Terence did not answer, continued to stare at the object in the palm of his outstretched hand, something that, in the light of the torch, he recognised instantly.

'So Malcolm did come down here,' he said in an oddly hushed voice. 'This tie-pin. I sent it to him three years ago for his birthday!'

'This is obviously where he gained most of the knowledge to construct those designs in his room,' nodded Park without looking up. He continued to write feverishly, covering page after page with symbols and diagrams. At length he straightened, thrust the notepad into his pocket. Taking the torch from the vicar, he played the beam around the walls of the cyclopean structure.

It was difficult to estimate how far below ground level they were, possibly more than a hundred feet and not a single ray of light penetrated to those stygian depths where the smell of must and decay had lain undisturbed for centuries.

'I suppose this must have been used as some kind of dungeon in the old days,' Ventnor said in a faint voice, staring about him in the gloom. 'In those unsettled times, the de Grinleys must have had a lot of enemies.'

'I strongly suspect that around the time of Hubert de Grinley and those who came after him, it was used for far more terrible purposes than that.' Park was moving unsteadily forward as he spoke, the torchlight now fixed on one particular part of the wall. He paused in front of it, holding the torch close to the stone. 'Take a look at this.'

Amberley peered over the other's shoulder. There was a pile of debris at the base of the wall at this point and as he looked closer he was able to follow the outlines of what had once been a large archway but had been completely blocked up in some bygone time.

'I wonder . . . ' Park stepped back a little, glancing over his shoulder in the direction from which they had just come. 'If I remember correctly, we were facing east when we came down those steps at the top. They led straight down into that first chamber and there was then a right-angled turn to the left and we've moved straight on since then, which means that the tunnel, or whatever it is which lies beyond this arch leads due north from the village.'

Amberley tensed at the implication behind the other's words. 'You mean?'

'I mean that the chances are there is — or was at some time — a connecting tunnel between here and Cranston's Hill. We should have guessed at this possibility. A secret way for the de Grinleys to arrive at the point of sacrifice.'

The vicar frowned. 'But this place must be almost a mile from Cranston's Hill. It would have been a monumental task to dig a tunnel of that length in those days.'

'Perhaps, But neither impossible nor unheard of. Even the neolithic peoples used to excavate such warrens in the hills. All that troubles me at the moment is who blocked it up — and why.'

'Almost certainly the villagers when they rioted against that accursed family,' said Ventnor.

'A logical explanation,' agreed Park, 'I only hope to God that it is the right one!'

8

Flight from Evil

It was just striking eleven p.m. when Terence opened the door to admit the vicar with the tall figure of Clivedon Park looming up behind him.

Earlier that afternoon, he had visited Anne, had told her a little of what had happened, of Park's fears, keeping back only enough to prevent her from being terrified. He had managed, in the end, to extract from her the promise that no matter what happened that night, no matter what she might see and hear, she was to remain indoors.

'You're sure you're ready to go through with this, Amberley?' asked Park as the other closed the door behind them. 'I want you both to clearly understand that the precautions I've provided us with may not be sufficiently strong to overcome this evil force which we are about to face.'

'I'm ready,' Terence said, forcing evenness into his voice. 'I've come this far and if it will explain how and why Malcolm died I intend to go through with it.'

'Good man,' nodded the other. He gestured towards the stairs. 'I think we should go upstairs where we can keep a watch on the road at the end of the lane.'

They made their way upstairs and into the bedroom where Park took up his station at the window. On his instructions, the light was put out and they sat in the clinging darkness staring out into the night. The sky was clear with only a few scattered clouds, which blotted out the stars at intervals. The moon, almost near new, would not rise until shortly before dawn and they could expect no light from it.

It was impossible to tell when the sound first began for it seemed to have been there for several minutes before the ear registered it and it began to play on their senses. Terence found himself gripping the ledge of the window convulsively, fingers tightening of their own accord.

One glance at the dimly-seen faces of his companions told him that they, too, were experiencing the weird sensation.

Swiftly, the fear that had been crystallising in his mind reached a crescendo. There were still several lights showing in the cluster of houses at the far end of the lane and more than once he found himself turning his head sharply to stare at the skyline where the rounded hump of Cranston's Hill lifted from the fields in the distance, half expecting to witness that same red, hellish glow he had noticed the last time this eerie muted throbbing had occurred, but as yet it loomed in total darkness with no sign of anything out of the ordinary.

'I don't think it will be long now,' murmured Park, craning his neck.

'What are you expecting to happen?' asked the vicar hoarsely.

'You'll see shortly,' was the only reply he got.

A quarter of an hour passed. As they stood there, Terence was acutely aware of his heart hammering against his ribs, its normal rhythm speeding up as the tension continued to mount in the room.

'Ah!' Park uttered the single word almost explosively in a hiss of indrawn breath.

'What is it?' Terence peered out and saw almost immediately that the lights in the houses were flicking out, were being extinguished one by one as if at a pre-arranged signal. At the same time the throbbing vibration grew stronger, great eddying waves that pulsed and beat all around them. He fingered the crucifix that hung about his neck with shaking fingers. The urge to get to his feet and go out into the night grew in his mind, not as strong nor as insistent as on that previous occasion, but perceptible all the same.

A sudden movement attracted his attention. A dark figure emerged from the shadows of the houses at the end of the lane. As he watched it was joined by another. He thought he recognised Doctor Harmon there and another shape, leaning on a stick, hobbling along the main road leading north out of Tormount that could only have been the bent frame of Lady Parrish. This could not possibly be happening, his mind screamed silently at him. This was some dream, some nightmarish illusion brought on by the experiences of the past few days.

But then came the rush of fear as he watched the slow procession file out into the star-glimmering night, never once slackening their speed as they moved along the road between the tall hedges bordering the fields.

An eternity seemed to elapse as they stood there at the window, watching until the last of the vague shapes had vanished around the bend in the road less than a quarter of a mile away. Then Clivedon Park moved away from the window, abruptly breaking the spell that seemed to have gripped them.

With an oddly dazed movement, Terence followed the others to the door, down the creaking stairs, and out of the front door into the throbbing night. By the time they reached the end of the winding lane, the road that stretched away before them was empty, deserted.

'We must hurry now,' said Park tersely.

'And remember — when we get to the top of Cranston's Hill, whatever you see or hear, do exactly as I say. If we should be discovered, or even if our presence should only be suspected, they may either try to attack us on an occult level, or on a merely physical level. If we should have to flee, don't let anything stop you. Try to forget that those people up there are your friends. They are acting now under the influence of something terribly evil. They don't know what they are doing. Tomorrow morning, they will probably have forgotten all about this, would not even believe you if you confronted them with any concrete evidence.'

Terence, as he fell into step beside the others was seized by a niggling feeling of unreality. He had heard how people could be hypnotised to do things completely alien to their character, and yet know nothing about it when they were finally snapped out of their hypnotic trance. But this seemed to be mass hypnotism on so vast a scale that it was utterly unbelievable. People like the much respected and revered Lady Parrish, scarcely able to walk unaided, moving with the rest of these men and women, up towards the Standing Stones to take part in some unholy ceremony.

Now they were walking through the tall trees which grew on either side of the road and there seemed to be a curious kind of stirring among the branches and leaves which was not quite like the sound of animals or the footsteps of human beings. There was something out there, all around them, something that had them fixed with a hard and implacable hatred, watching their every movement, completely aware of them.

It was perhaps twenty minutes later that Park halted, looked about him, then motioned to their right. 'We'd better strike across country now,' he said, keeping his voice down. 'They may have someone watching the road although I don't consider it likely.'

Flicking the torch on for a fraction of a second, he shone it towards the tall hedge. A few yards further along there was a gate leading into the field. Fumbling a little in the darkness, he unfastened the latch and swung it open. Beneath their feet, the soft ground squelched loudly. They were making far too much noise, Terence thought in a sudden frenzy. Someone was bound to hear them.

Ahead of them, over the fields, long, thin tendrils of mist oozed up from the moist ground. Away from the road, it seemed the mist grew thicker and all pervading, and soon they were in the midst of it, clammy fingers coiling all around them. The murmur of water came from somewhere near at hand and a moment later they were forced to jump a narrow stream.

Now their route lay directly ahead and they walked slowly on with Park in the lead, the mist, dense in places providing them with sufficient concealment to enable them to move more quickly than before in spite of the impeding roots and thorn bushes that loomed up in their path without warning.

The throbbing in the air now beat down at them; compulsive, threatening, summoning and warning. They continued on across three more fields, the ground underfoot growing more wild and desolate as they progressed and gradually it began to rise steeply.

Terence realised they had reached the foot of Cranston's Hill, approaching it from the east. Here they were forced to move more slowly and cautiously, their way barred by stinking pools of water which had collected on the lower slopes and all the time they climbed over the craggy outcrops of rock, they were aware of dim, unseen presences which seemed to be moving with them, just at the edge of their vision, never once coming out into the open.

They had now clambered above the level of the writhing mist and for the first time he grew aware of the palely flickering glow that came from directly above them.

Just what was going on up there among the ring of Standing Stones he did not know, but there was evil here. He could feel it in the air, soaking through every pore in his body. There was a smell too, like the stench of the Pit, clogging the back of his nostrils until it was difficult to breathe.

The choking growth of creeping roots and thick, fleshy, abnormal growths thinned now and they were forced to worm their way forward on hands and knees, the razor-edged rocks cutting into their flesh.

Reaching a huddle of low, stunted bushes, they settled themselves there and peered about them on all sides. Then, as Terence lifted his head a little to get a better view, the most terrible impression was borne in upon him — a sight that gripped him in a vice of absolute terror, The paralysis of utter fear held him rigid in that instant. Every nerve and fibre locked tight in a spasmodic grip, he could only crouch there and watch.

There was a sharp rock digging into the palm of his hand where he was resting the whole of his weight on it, but he was not aware of the pain lancing through his flesh. Beside him, he felt the vicar shiver convulsively for a long moment. From all about him, there rose the stench of rottenness and decay, the smell of earth and mould and rotting tissue.

Eerie and frightening beyond all description, the pale reddish glow pervaded the whole of the scene, lighting the carved columns of the Standing Stones, touching the faces of the men and women gathered there in a great circle inside the ring of rough-hewn columns, It was like looking out upon a scene from Dante's Inferno.

Only vaguely was he aware that the mind-rending vibration had ceased, suddenly and abruptly. There was a curious, absolute silence. In the hush he could hear his heart beating furiously. The red glow seemed to reach far back beyond the hilltop, touching deep and endless avenues of benighted blackness, hinting at dim shapes in the dark shadows.

He saw the glare shine on the faces of the people of the village. Harmon and Ralph Treherne standing side by side on the far edge of the clearing. Little Miss Munderford, the post-mistress whose wild tale had scarcely been believed. Lady Parrish and many others he recognised. Small wonder that they had tried to dissuade him from digging any further into this mystery, why they had wanted him to believe that Malcolm had died by his own hand, so that he would leave and they could work their evil here undisturbed.

He felt the urge to turn and run for this was madness of the most diabolical kind. The vicar's body too was straining for flight, trying to tear itself from Park's grasp. The other had turned his head now to look at each of them in turn and in that grim countenance Terence found little comfort, little assurance that the knowledge that this man supposedly possessed would be sufficient, would be strong enough to overcome this devilish force.

There was a sudden movement on the very rim of the circle of light. Terence felt the blood drain from his face as he saw who it was. Slowly, laboriously, the figure moved forward, the limbs jerking and twitching like those of a puppet activated by strings, held by some evil master, responding to his every command.

It was Malcolm!

Slowly, the figure advanced through the circle of men and women, walked stiffly and mechanically to the centre of the

Standing Stones. The arms lifted suddenly, the dead body stiffened.

The sudden appearance of the other seemed to break the spell that had held a tight grip on Terence's mind. He was able to move again — yet he remained quite still, breathing heavily, forcing the air in and out of his lungs with a conscious, physical effort.

Dark and tall, seemingly larger than life in the red glare, the figure remained poised in the centre of the ring and now there came a weird and undulating chant from the watchers, it rose and fell in a cadence that was both horrible and frightening. Nothing more could surely happen now, he thought frenziedly. He did not even begin to convince himself. This was merely the beginning of the horror. Worse was still to come.

There was a shimmering of mist, oozing out of the ground, out of that blasted spot where nothing grew, where the ancient Altar of Belial once had rested. Straining his eyes, the blood pounding through his forehead, Terence watched as the mist curdled and thickened, took on a definite shape; a shape both frightening and familiar. A nauseous odour seeped up from the ground and threatened to engulf them all.

From what terrible gulf of time that thing had been drawn, Terence Amberley could not even begin to guess. Monstrous in outline, yet oddly human, it stood poised in front of the thing that had once been his brother; the same thing he had glimpsed in that room at the top of the house, inside the pentacle drawn on the dusty floor.

Waves of pure evil emanated from it, sweeping over them as they crouched in the darkness just beyond that hellish glare. Man or devil, it was impossible to tell.

Terence breathed in horror as he felt the numbness seeping into his limbs. Beside him, he grew aware that Park had commenced to mutter through his tightly clenched teeth. The words were at first indistinguishable, but gradually Terence recognised that they were Latin and even as he watched, the other had leapt to his feet, the silver crucifix on its long chain, held out before him as he began to advance slowly towards that terrible monstrosity which had somehow been called up from the depths of the Pit.

There was a kind of bluish haze and a weird spluttering and for a moment it was as if the creature shrank back, dimmed a little. There was a cracking sound in the air, but whether it came from around him or was merely inside his own head, Terence could not say.

The repulsive figure reared up, seemed to grow larger than before, looming over the shape of Clivedon Park as he struggled to force his way forward, the long body, bent at the waist as if fighting some terrible, unseen force, strangely diminutive before that vast, rearing shape in the clearing.

Fearfully, Terence could only crouch and watch, aware that the vicar too was murmuring something under his breath. Then he saw that the dimness of that hellish glow was not real but only one of contrast. Shadowy and monstrous, the battle continued for several seconds but even to Terence's numbed mind it became apparent that evil was winning. Slowly, Park was being forced back.

There came a sudden roar as if from a thousand throats, a yell of demoniac triumph.

Then, with a sharp motion, a flick of his arm, Park hurled the cross straight into the devilish face which leered down at him. There was a blinding flash and when Terence could see properly again, the hideous monstrosity had vanished in a swirling of vapour and there was only the terrible stench still hanging in the air.

Clivedon Park came staggering back. His face seemed white and bloodless. Sweat lay in a sheen on his forehead.

'Quickly!' he gasped, half falling against the portly shape of the vicar. 'We have to get back to the village. Hurry. There's very little time.'

'But it's gone,' muttered Ventnor harshly. 'We've beaten it. Sent it back where it belongs.'

'No!' Park snapped. 'That isn't true. I've been a fool. I should have realised it before. There is only one way to stop this abomination now. We have to find the body of Richard de Grinley and I think I know where it is.' He had veered down the narrow, tortuous path now, his right hand gripping Terence's sleeve.

From somewhere behind them, there was the sound of movement, of wild cries, more animal-like than human. As he ran, stumbling over the rough, rocky ground, Terence threw a swift glance over his shoulder.

Behind them came a stream of humanity. There was no mistaking the intentions of those men and women.

The evil force had been beaten back, but only on the one plane. This attack, as Park had prophesied, was to be on a purely physical level. That evil entity which had been the reincarnation of Richard de Grinley, must have realised its danger. Now the thought had been implanted in the minds of these people that they had to be killed, or at any rate stopped, from continuing the battle.

In a series of wild, danger-filled leaps, they reached the bottom of the rock-strewn slope. Ventnor was puffing and wheezing now. Splashing through the deep puddles, the water soaking their legs, they ran with leaden legs, driving themselves to the utmost physical limit of their bodies. Several times, Ventnor staggered and fell, gasping with the agony as the two men beside him hauled him roughly to his feet and pulled him on. There was the crashing of heavy bodies pushing through the stunted bushes and trees and now the sound seemed to come to the side of them also, as if a party of the villagers were heading for the main road in an attempt to cut them off from the village.

Park reached a sudden decision as he too heard the sound and recognised its import. 'They know where we are,' he rapped harshly. 'We shall have to go across the fields. A quick break. First we must get to the rectory. It's our only hope.'

Swaying like drunken men, they ran blindly through the wet grass and all the time they ran it was as if noiseless, unseen things passed through the air above their heads, riding the wind, following them. Thorns scored their flesh, tearing at their clothing. Their legs were like lead, lanced through with spasms of pain. Ahead of them, seemingly still far away in the distance, they could just make out the square tower of the church silhouetted against the starlit night. Beside it, the rectory stood in darkness.

The sound of their pursuers was very close now, less than two hundred yards away. Hampered by the treacherous nature of the ground, the long, straight furrows over which they had been forced to run, it had been possible for those villagers running along the main road to draw almost level with them.

There would be no escape if they managed to swing around, block their route to the rectory, although what hope they would have even if they did succeed in reaching it before the others, Terence could not guess. If all of their efforts back there on top of Cranston's Hill had failed, what more could they hope for here? And where under the stars was the body of Richard de Grinley?

A turmoil of half-formed thoughts roared through his brain as he ran. Out of the corner of his eye, he saw the clustered mass of dark figures break into view at the edge of the village, saw them pause for a moment as they looked about them, obviously searching for their victims. Instantly, the three men froze in their tracks, gasping harshly.

'They haven't seen us yet,' Park whispered, 'but they'll guess where we are headed. We shall have to go through the churchyard, and at the moment, much of their evil power could be concentrated there. But it's a risk we will have to take.'

Leading the way, he moved to his left, away from the direction of the road, towards the narrow gap in the high hedge. Over everything now loomed the great stone tower of the church. Surely here they ought to be safe from evil, Terence thought. Unless, in the past, the church had been used for services other than Christian . . .

They picked their way slowly among the canted gravestones, moving from one concealing shadow to the next, circling the great mass of the church itself until they came upon the tiny path that led into the garden of the rectory. Cautiously, they made their way along it.

There came a vaguely muffled shouting

from the direction of the village street. Another shout answered from a different direction. It was as though they were completely surrounded.

'There may still be time for what we have to do,' Park said hurriedly. 'First, Vicar, we shall need holy water. This thing we have to lay to rest is down in that accursed vault under the manor. Think you could go through with it?'

'I think so,' answered the other shakily. 'But there is no need to go to the rectory? I have holy water in the church.'

Turning, he pulled a large key from his pocket and led the way to the heavy iron door. Unlocking it, he pushed it open on creaking hinges and led the way inside.

Standing in the cool darkness of the church, Terence felt a strange sense of peace after the terror and the pandemonium of the past hour.

The vicar was gone only a few minutes. When he returned, he carried a tiny flask and a black-bound book.

'I'm ready,' he said quietly and to Terence it seemed that there was a new note of confidence in his tone.

In the darkness, the place was positively ghoulish-looking. Even the torch in Park's hand could only illuminate a little of the ruins at any one time and on all sides, the blackness seemed more than absolute, holding a waiting quality of supercharged menace. Carefully, they let themselves down into the narrow passage at the base of the fallen, splintered stone columns of the old manor.

There was still some confused yelling in the distance but most of it seemed centered around the church and the rectory and somehow they had managed to slip through any cordon that may have been thrown around the place, without incident.

Amberley followed closely behind Park. Like a descent into some hideous, haunted well, the passage led them on, floundering ahead with faltering steps.

Eventually, they reached the burial chamber and for a moment, Park played the light from the torch over the boxes ranged along the walls but there was nothing out of the ordinary there and they seemed to have been undisturbed. Down the even steeper, darker passage at the far end and into that terrible inner chamber and now Terence felt his fear beginning to get the better of him. The overpowering sense of evil foreboding struck at him like the force of a physical blow as he felt his feet touch the level ground at the bottom of the passage.

Was the holy water they had brought with them sufficient to defeat the powers of darkness, which Malcolm, in his ignorance, seemed to have put in motion? And if they failed, what then? Park had spoken of a fate much worse than death itself and now, in the whispering blackness, the words struck home to him.

Clivedon Park did not hesitate. Keeping a tight grip on the torch, he advanced towards the massive grey shape of the altar reposing in the middle of the chamber. Then he paused and turned to the others.

'We've got to find the way to remove the top of this altar,' he said harshly. 'There has to be a way.'

'But — ' began Ventnor, puzzled.

'Don't you see?' demanded the other, his eyes blazing fiercely. 'There is no record of when or how Richard de Grinley died.'

'The legend says that he never did die,' Terence put in hoarsely.

'It wasn't until we were on top of the hill that it came to me what the legend meant.' Park was speaking eagerly now, almost in a frenzy. 'This is where he's buried. Inside the Altar of Belial. That is why he swore he would never die so long as it remained within the boundaries of the parish, why it was brought here. Out there among the Standing Stones it was too vulnerable. It had to be brought somewhere safe. What we saw on Cranston's Hill tonight was the evil entity that was Richard de Grinley. His bones are inside this stone sarcophagus.'

Even as he spoke, he was moving slowly around the massive slab of stone, holding the torch in one hand and feeling along the stone with the fingertips of his other.

Slowly, he made his way around it, then paused, uttered an exclamation of satisfaction. 'Just as I thought.' He pressed one of the tiny carvings.

Nothing visible happened, but a faint rumble came from somewhere seemingly deep within the stone mass.

'Give me a hand. Both of you,' he commanded. Resting the torch on the ground, he seized the edge of the altar and began to push with all of his strength, teeth clenched tightly. Terence hesitated briefly, then threw his own weight against the lid of the stone. For a long moment, nothing happened. Then slowly, ponderously, the slab on top of the altar began to move, grinding across the base.

He sucked in a deep gust of air, shuddered at the stench that rose into his nostrils. An inch at a time, the lid of the altar moved, grating sideways with a leaden motion.

Then, abruptly, there was another sound within the confining walls of the chamber, or rather it came from outside. The sweat streaming down his face with the exertion, Terence straightened sharply. For several seconds, it was impossible to guess from which direction this new sound came. His first thought was that some of the villagers had somehow plucked up sufficient courage to follow them into the ruins but then, as his thoughts orientated themselves, he realised that this was not so.

The sound came from the other side of the vast chamber, *from behind that blocked up arch that they had discovered that morning*!

'What is it?' muttered the vicar, wiping the perspiration from his face with the back of his hand.

'Some of them must have worked their way along that tunnel from the hill.' For a second, there was a note almost of fear in Clivedon Park's voice. He picked up the torch and flashed it on the wall in the direction of the tall archway. Even from where they stood, it was just possible to make out the wide cracks that were appearing in the wall. Quite clearly it had not been blocked by stone as they had thought, but merely dried mud with some smaller stones mixed with it.

Desperation now gave them added strength. Gripping the stone slab in both hands, they thrust with all of their might and slowly, it ground its way over the top of the huge altar, finally tilting on the far side and toppling to the floor with a resounding crash.

'All right, Vicar. You know what you have to do,' snapped Park. He stepped to the end of the altar, flashed the torch momentarily into the gaping black opening that leered before them. Flashing it only for a few seconds to reveal what lay inside.

His face was impassive as one who has seen too much horror in his lifetime as to be steeled against it, but there was a tiny muscle twitching high in his right cheek and his eyes closed momentarily as he stepped back a pace. Deliberately he switched off the torch, leaving the vicar in the darkness. But he did not do it quickly enough to prevent Terence from catching a glimpse of the body that lay there in that great stone coffin. That it was the remains of Richard de Grinley, he did not doubt; yet there came a sharp surge of vomit into his mouth at the sight of the skeleton that lay there, dressed in what had once been rich wrappings of silk.

It was not the bones so much that brought the terror welling up inside him, nor even the grinning skull that leered at him from sightless sockets. Rather it was the fragmentary glimpse he had seen of the two five-inch horns that grew out of the forehead.

The Devil Incarnate as the old legends would have it — or some terrible freak of nature, the last in the line of a degenerate family?

Hesitantly at first, but with his voice gaining strength with each succeeding second, the vicar began to pronounce the words of absolution, at the same time sprinkling the holy water from the flask over the interior of the coffin.

Scarcely had he begun to do so than a terrible scream of demoniacal fury seemed to fill the chamber, echoing and re-echoing back from the looming walls on either side.

Then, abruptly, there was silence, deep and final and when Clivedon Park finally summoned up the courage to turn on the torch once more and shine it into the coffin, there was nothing there but a small pile of white dust that eddied greyly over the once rich brocade.

* * *

There were still some bees murmuring among the chrysanthemums in the sharp, cool sunlight the following afternoon. Yet now there seemed to be a very different atmosphere over the entire village, as if some terrible, cancerous growth had been removed.

That morning, the vicar had driven Clivedon Park back to Nottingham in his wheezing old Ford and now Terence Amberley was standing here with Anne beside him, looking out over a village that seemed to have come to life after having been in some dark and nightmare-haunted sleep for a hundred years.

It still seemed incredible that no one recalled anything of what had happened the previous night or on the other nights when they had left the village in answer to a summons they could not resist and had gone up there to Cranston's Hill, now slumbering in the afternoon sunshine, and taken part in the most diabolical rituals.

A small group of men had gone out to the Standing Stones on the vicar's instructions early that morning and there they had found the body of Malcolm Amberley, lying almost as it had been found before. But this time, so they had told Terence, it was as if he had died peacefully in his sleep, almost with a smile on his face. He would be buried again in the quiet grave beside the church.

Anne glanced up at him, wondering a little at his long silence, then linked her arm through his. 'You still haven't told me what happened last night,' she said softly. 'I know something did because everyone is — well, somehow different — today.'

'There isn't much to tell,' he said gently. 'Just let's say that the evil which once existed is no more. Malcolm is dead, but he can rest in peace now.'

'And you. What are you going to do now? Go back to London?'

'For a little while,' he said, almost

regretfully. 'I have to. But I think I'd like to come and live in a place like this where everything is so peaceful and time doesn't seem to matter at all.'

'I'm sure you would be doing the right thing if you did come back and live here. It seems that house there has known so much evil, it needs a chance to live again.'

They walked slowly down the winding lane, between the fields over which the sunlight hung like a golden curtain. At the corner, where they were hidden from the village, he put his arms around her slim waist, kissed her on the lips, feeling her respond. Now this, he thought, was the first wonderful thing that had happened to him since he had arrived in the village.

THE END